HEARTSIDE
BAY

THE **HEARTSIDE BAY** SERIES

HEARTSIDE BAY

Kiss at Midnight

CATHY COLE

■SCHOLASTIC

Scholastic Children's Books
An imprint of Scholastic Ltd
Euston House, 24 Eversholt Street, London, NW1 1DB, UK
Registered office: Westfield Road, Southam, Warwickshire, CV47 0RA
SCHOLASTIC and associated logos are trademarks and/or
registered trademarks of Scholastic Inc.

First published in the UK by Scholastic Ltd, 2014

Text copyright © Scholastic Ltd, 2014

ISBN 978 1407 14051 3

A CIP catalogue record for this book
is available from the British Library.

Printed and bound by CPI Group (UK) Ltd, Croydon, CR0 4YY
Papers used by Scholastic Children's Books are made
from wood grown in sustainable forests.

1 3 5 7 9 10 8 6 4 2

www.scholastic.co.uk

Merci beaucoup to Lucy Courtenay
and Sara Grant

ONE

The moon shone on the flickering waves as the motorcycle screamed along the coast road. Lila Murray clung tightly to the leather jacket in front of her and leaned back so that she could see the stars. They were bright tonight.

"You're not serious," Polly had said earlier that night. Her hazel eyes looked worried below her deep brown fringe as she watched the tall, long-haired guy shrugging on his battered leather jacket in the door of the café. "You don't even know the guy's name, and you're accepting lifts?"

"I know he has a motorcycle," Lila had giggled, grabbing her coat from the café table. "And he's hot. Don't be so serious, Polly. It's the holidays, and I want some fun. Tell him to wait, will you? I need to fix my make-up."

She had dashed into the ladies to fix her eyeliner and pinch some colour into her pale cheeks. Her wide blue eyes were a little bloodshot – she hadn't been sleeping too well lately – and her hair hadn't been brushed in a while, but it still looked good. She decided she liked it though. It was a bit rock and roll.

Polly had been waiting for her outside. "Lila, I really don't think—" she began.

Lila brushed past. Polly meant well but she could be a real bore. "I can look after myself, Pol," she said, wriggling into her coat. "We only have one life and I'm going to live mine to the full, if that's OK with you."

Up close the motorcycle was huge. Lila swallowed her nerves. She smiled flirtatiously at the motorcycle driver, and accepted the helmet he handed her.

This will be fun, she promised herself as she climbed aboard.

The leather-jacketed stranger on the seat in front of her felt warm and solid. Scenting freedom on the wind, Lila felt a little life seeping back into her bones as the bike roared away from the café. Soon Polly was nothing but a lonely speck in the rear-view mirror.

Lila felt a little bad abandoning her friend. But she soon lost herself in imagining the excitement of the adventure that lay ahead of her.

She lost track of the rest of the evening. They had driven for miles, she knew that much. There had been a spectacular sunset, which they had watched from the top of Smugglers' Hill. Her date didn't say much, but he was a reasonably good kisser. That was fine by Lila. She didn't feel much like talking.

On the way back to Heartside Bay, Lila had reached up to take her helmet off as the road tore away beneath the wheels of the bike. She wanted to feel the wind in her hair, the way she had felt it on her face and hands. But she realized she wasn't brave enough. Visions of Ryan leaping off that cliff to his death flashed through her mind, as they so often did.

Any time her life started to feel normal again – happy even – the guilt and grief of Ryan's death always came crashing back. She hadn't even liked him but she'd led him on, and then he'd died. She wanted so badly to feel alive and carefree. But even this exciting, dangerous, secret, late-night ride with a handsome stranger had failed to bring that feeling with it. Instead, all she felt was a kind of numbness.

Ryan's death had killed something inside her. She had never lost anyone like that. He was there one minute, laughing and clowning around, and the next. . .

He's gone, she thought with a shiver. It was still impossible to believe.

She clung more tightly to the driver, leaning as the bike dipped around a corner. The lights of Heartside Bay were twinkling straight ahead of them now, spread out around the heart-shaped bay that gave the town its name. Lila's sense of freedom suddenly felt like a struggling fish on a line, being reeled in and left to gasp for breath on the quayside.

For one mad moment she felt like telling the driver to keep going.

The motorcycle pulled up outside the Ciao Café on the High Street and spluttered to a stop. It was late, and the silence of the evening was deafening.

The driver pulled off his helmet and ran his hands through his long and tangled hair. Lila forgot everything else as she looked into his handsome face. She slowly pulled off her helmet and smiled flirtatiously at him.

"Great ride," she said. She still didn't know his name. It didn't really matter. She wouldn't see him again.

He raised his eyebrows. "Is that all the thanks I get?"

Lila fluffed up her hair and pulled him towards her for a long, deep kiss. It wasn't as exciting as the earlier kisses had been but it was better than nothing.

"Better?" she enquired as she let him go.

"Much better," he said, coming back for another kiss.

Lila held him off. "I have to go."

He looked disappointed. "Don't leave me. The evening's hardly begun."

His eyes were almost black, with long eyelashes that swept his smooth cheeks. He really was gorgeous.

"How about we head to the beach?" he murmured, holding her a little more tightly as he sensed her hesitation.

Lila pictured the beach, the waves crashing on the shore. She wound her hands through his long dark hair

5

and kissed him again, with some desperation this time. Anything to push away the image of Ryan lying face down in those self-same waves.

It didn't work. She pulled back, wanting to cry with frustration.

"I have to go home," she mumbled.

"I'll call you," he said, catching at her hands.

Lila's heart sank. Why had she given him her number? *That* was a mistake she wouldn't make again.

"Sure," she said, backing away from him. "See you around."

She walked quickly away down the High Street, turning right a little sooner than necessary. She could sense him watching her, and it made her uncomfortable.

She made several unnecessary lefts and rights through the Old Town. It was stupid, but it made her feel safer. She clutched her coat around her and shivered as she passed the Heartbeat Café. Ryan's presence was strong here, outside the café owned by his parents.

She checked her watch as she turned into her road. Half past midnight. OK, so she had a curfew these days for past misdemeanours, but she felt reasonably confident that her parents wouldn't have noticed her absence tonight. If she could get into the house without being seen, she might get away with it.

Avoiding the creaking step halfway up the stairs, Lila made it into her dark bedroom without making a sound. Shutting the door carefully behind her, she exhaled with relief. Success.

Shaking out her hair and pulling off her coat, she flipped on the lights.

"Which part about an eleven o'clock curfew do you not understand, Lilian?"

Lila spun round, her heart thundering with shock.

Her parents were sitting side by side on her bed with their arms folded. Her mother looked sad. Her dad on the other hand looked absolutely furious.

TWO

Lila's father stood up.

"This has to stop, Lila," he said.

Lila tried to calm her breathing. She couldn't show any weakness. Her father was trained to sniff out weakness in the criminals that he arrested. She wouldn't give him an inch.

"I'm home now, aren't I?" she said, hanging up her coat. "You don't have to make such a fuss about it."

"Don't speak to your father like that," said her mum.

Lila shrugged. "I need to go to the bathroom," she said.

Her father barred her way, leaning his hand on the bedroom door. "You know where this is heading, don't you? Back down that long, slippery slide of trouble you landed yourself in when we lived in London. We moved here to leave that behind us, remember?"

Lila remembered London with an ache in her throat. She hadn't known Ryan then. She had never seen death. For all its problems, London suddenly looked like paradise. She wished bitterly they had never come to Heartside Bay.

"You have been coming in all hours of the night despite the perfectly reasonable curfew we ask of you," said her mother. "You've been moody and disrespectful for weeks now. Like your father says, this has to stop."

Lila could feel the tears building behind her eyes. Why did everyone make her cry all the time? She was just trying to make the most of her life, now that she'd come to realize how short and unpredictable it could be.

"Can I go to the bathroom now?" she said.

"We have tried to be patient," her father continued. His hand was still on the door, barring her escape. "We know how upset you've been about Ryan's death. Something senseless like this affects everyone in this community. But life goes on. We all have to make the best of what we have. This behaviour can't continue Lila."

Lila blinked away the image of Ryan in the waves. It seemed to haunt her every waking moment. "Leave me alone," she said in a shaking voice.

She pulled at her bedroom door.

"This hasn't been easy for us either," said her mother a little more gently. "Your father has known Mr Jameson since they were children. They grew up together, went to school together. It's terrible, watching your friends grieve and being unable to help."

Lila clenched her fists. When would this stop? She'd had a great evening, and now all she wanted to do was go to sleep. Her parents seemed determined to stop her.

"Please leave my bedroom," she said through gritted teeth. "I want to go to sleep."

"Busy evening?" her father enquired.

There was something barbed in his tone of voice that made Lila look up.

"Yeah a bit," she said warily.

"Who were you with?"

"You can't help interrogating people, can you Dad?" Lila shot at him. "Just because you're a police officer at work, doesn't give you the right to act like one at home."

"Who were you with, Lila?" her father repeated in a steelier tone.

Lila tossed her hair back. "I was with Polly, if you must know," she said. Polly would cover for her, she decided. That's what friends were for.

"Please don't lie to us, Lila," said her mother, shaking her head. "It only makes matters worse. Someone saw you jump on the back of a motorcycle this afternoon. To our knowledge, Polly Nelson doesn't ride a motorcycle."

Lila flinched. Was nothing in this town private? She hated the way everyone knew each other's business. She couldn't believe some busybody had seen her and reported back to her parents! She felt stifled, smothered . . . angry.

Angry was good, she realized. It was a *feeling*, at least.

"You can't possibly understand what I'm going through!" she shouted, using her anger like a weapon. "I wish we'd never left London!"

"We left London for you, Lila," said her father.

Lila started pummelling at her father's chest. "I hate you!" she screamed. Deep down she knew this kind of behaviour would only land her in more trouble, but she didn't care. "I hate this town! I can't believe you brought me here!"

"It's easy to blame others, isn't it?" said her father harshly. "It means you don't have to look too closely at yourself."

Lila didn't want to look too closely at herself. She knew what she would see: Ryan, Ryan, always Ryan. She flung herself on to her bed, her arms tightly folded across her body.

"You can't keep me in here for ever," she said defiantly.

"We know that," said her mother. She looked pale and anxious.

"To make matters worse," her father said, looking even more serious, "we received a call from school this afternoon."

"Whoopee," said Lila, fighting with every ounce of her being not to cry. "Let's hang out some flags."

"Your grades have slipped to an unacceptable level, Lila. Messing up at school *and* at home?"

Lila felt winded. "Big deal," she said aloud as if she couldn't care less. "What does school matter anyway?"

"What does it *matter*?" said her father incredulously. "Don't you realize what a tough world it is out there? You need qualifications! And at the rate you're going, you won't get any. So your mother and I have made a decision."

Her mother was standing with her father now. A united front, Lila realized with a sinking heart. This was going to be bad.

"Starting on Monday," her father went on, "you will spend two hours each morning with a tutor for the entire holiday, revising and getting up to speed with your work before next term begins."

Lila was so shocked, she couldn't speak. A *tutor*?

"What?" she managed. "I'm not spending my holiday with some bad-breath geek telling me how to do stuff, Dad. That's just embarrassing!"

Her father looked unmoved. "You should have thought of that before you let it get to this level, Lila. Two hours a day. Non-negotiable. And if you don't start meeting curfew and treating your mother and me with some more respect, we will have to consider a more severe punishment. You're on thin ice right now Lila. Don't disappoint us any more than you have already." He opened the door. "You can go to the bathroom now."

Lila slammed the bathroom door so hard her toothbrush slid into the sink with a clatter. She leaned her head against the wood and closed her eyes.

What is the point? she thought in absolute despair. Good grades hadn't made a difference when Ryan jumped off that cliff. She had tried the whole good-girl thing when they had moved here, just like her parents wanted – and look what happened.

It wasn't even worth trying.

THREE

Lila woke groggily at the sound of buzzing near her head. She yawned and felt around for her phone on her bedside table.

It was a message from Rhi.

Meet at the Heartbeat
12 noon xx

Lila remembered with a pang how she had hurried past the Heartbeat last night, creeped out by the memories of Ryan. She and her friends hadn't been to their favourite hang-out since Ryan had died. In fact now she thought about it, she could have sworn it was still closed. There were even rumours that the Jamesons were thinking of selling the place because they couldn't bear the memories. Lila knew how they felt. Why did Rhi want to meet there?

She checked the time at the top of the phone screen. Ten-thirty. She didn't have much time.

Thought the Heartbeat was still closed?

She pressed send and got out of bed, heading towards the bathroom. By the time she came out again, her hair freshly washed and hanging in dark tangles down her back, Rhi's message was waiting.

Don't ask questions.
Just come xx

Lila'd had a restless night, filled with her usual bad dreams. Despite herself, she was intrigued by Rhi's mysterious attitude. A bit of mystery with her friends might be just what she needed to cheer her up.

"Where are you going?" her mother called as Lila took the stairs two at a time, grabbing her bag and slipping her phone into her pocket.

"Out," Lila replied. She took her key from where it lived on the hall table and slid it into her coat pocket.

"Don't be out late," said her mother, appearing at her study door.

"Mum, it's eleven-thirty in the morning," said Lila, doing her best not to roll her eyes. "I'm hardly going to be out 'late', am I?" She glanced around a little warily. "Where's Dad?"

"He was called into the station."

Lila was surprised. "But it's Saturday."

"Criminals don't care about weekends," her mother pointed out.

As she opened the door, Lila hesitated. She looked back over her shoulder at her mother. "Is Dad still mad?" she asked.

"He's trying not to be. Cut him some slack, will you? Come back at a reasonable time today. Maybe we could have supper together."

Lila fiddled with the door catch. She didn't like fighting with her parents, but she wasn't ready to cooperate just yet. "I'll think about it," she said gruffly, before letting herself out into the street.

Part of her knew her parents were doing their best. She wasn't easy at the moment, she knew that. But she shuddered to think about sitting round the table trying to make chit-chat with her dad. A day out with her friends was looking increasingly attractive.

Her phone rang as she turned down a cobbled lane into the Old Town.

"Hey, Rhi," said Lila, tucking her phone into her shoulder. "What's going on?"

"Spring clean," said Rhi. "Dad's going mad trying to work out where the Jamesons kept everything."

"What's your dad doing there?" Lila said in surprise.

"The Jamesons can't face running the café themselves yet, but they need the business. Dad's doing them a favour and taking on the lease for a couple of months. Starting tonight, he's going to run it for them until they work out what they want to do."

"What do you think they'll do?"

"Close it," said Rhi simply. "Unless we can figure out some way of making it so massively successful that they don't want to close it at all. That's the plan, basically. We need to come up with something to relaunch the Heartbeat on this town. If we don't, we'll probably lose it."

Lila was surprised at the lurch of sadness she felt deep in her belly. She didn't like even walking past the Heartbeat these days, let alone going inside. But she couldn't imagine Heartside Bay without it. The Heartbeat had always made their small-town life a bit more bearable with its live music, strong coffee and cosy parent-free atmosphere. She found herself wanting to help Rhi with this more than anything.

Lila hesitated on the pavement outside the café's battered wooden doors. It felt strange, preparing to go inside. Ryan stood on the pavement behind her, just out of sight. She knew he was there. She could feel him.

"We'll do our best, Ryan," she said out loud. "OK?" She pushed open the doors and went inside.

Polly rushed up to her at once, cleaning cloths dangling from her hands.

"Lila, were you OK last night? I was going mad, worrying about you. You didn't answer any of my texts."

Lila had deliberately turned off her phone last night

while she was with the boy on the motorcycle. It had been liberating, knowing that no one could contact her.

"You worry too much, Polly," she said out loud. "I was fine, just like I said I would be. He was really cute and really gentlemanly and we had a fantastic evening, OK?"

"Who was cute?" asked Rhi, looking round from straightening the bottles behind the bar.

"Biker Boy," said Polly testily.

"I met this guy last night," Lila explained as Rhi looked confused. "We went for a teensy ride on his motorcycle and had a few pretty average kisses. Polly thinks it's a much bigger deal than it really was."

Rhi looked upset. "Lila, that sounds dangerous!"

"Not you as well," Lila grumbled. "Lighten up, will you? I really got it in the neck from my parents last night when I got back, so I'd appreciate it if you didn't lay into me as well. Who has a cleaning cloth for me?"

"Plenty of cloths in the store cupboard," said Rhi's dad, appearing from behind the bar with a stack of crisp boxes balanced in his arms. "Help yourself. This place needs some serious sorting out."

It had been over three weeks since Ryan had died, and there were layers of dust on everything in the café: the coffee machine, the table tops, the chairs. The carpet looked dirty. Even the wooden walls with their messages of love inscribed into the panels down the generations were looking dull and sad.

"I never realized how run-down this place had got," Lila said, looking around.

Rhi wiped her head with the back of her hand. "When you're with your friends and the place is busy, you don't see the cracks."

"I've never seen it without people before," Polly said. "It's a little strange."

Rhi's dad put the crisps on the bar. "If we're going to get this place ready for opening tonight, we need to put our backs into it, girls. Tea break in an hour, OK?"

The girls worked hard through the afternoon, polishing and vacuuming, disinfecting the toilets and cleaning the little lead-pane windows. Generous helpings of furniture polish and a bit of elbow grease soon brought a fresh glow back to the scratched table tops and wooden walls.

If only you could achieve the same with life, Lila

thought wryly, polishing up their favourite table by the stage. *One spray and bam. Good as new.*

"Great!" Rhi's dad exclaimed when he saw what they had done. "I should get you girls over to help out more often. I think we're just about ready to open."

"Now all we need are the customers," said Polly. "Does anyone actually know the Heartbeat's opening again tonight?"

"I had an idea about that," Rhi said as they sat together on the stage with cups of tea and a packet of digestive biscuits Rhi's dad had brought along. "I'm going to ask Max to refresh the website and the Facebook page for the Heartbeat Café, to publicize Dad's new management. What do you think?"

Lila raised her eyebrows at the mention of Rhi's ex-boyfriend. "I didn't think you guys had talked to each other since you dumped him over the tannoy at the Funky Fox Festival."

"We haven't." Rhi fiddled with her mug. "But I'm sure he'll help if I ask him."

Lila noticed that Rhi was blushing. *Uh-oh*, she thought. She knew that look.

Polly knew it too. She leaned forward, fixing Rhi

with a stern eye. "Please don't tell me you're doing this just so you get Max to talk to you again, Rhi."

Rhi smiled weakly. "Maybe," she hedged, biting her lip.

Lila put her cup of tea down. "When will you learn, Rhi? You dumped him in front of ten thousand people. You guys aren't right for each other!"

"Lila is right," Polly added. "Don't do this."

"Why are you ganging up on me? I'm having second thoughts, what's wrong with that? I miss him. We've been together a long time. What if he's, you know . . . the one?" Rhi said.

Lila couldn't believe what she was hearing. As if there was such a thing as the perfect match for anyone – let alone at their age! "Come on, Rhi," she scoffed. "Everyone knows The One doesn't exist outside fairy tales and rom-coms."

"But what if he is?" Rhi persisted.

Lila had heard enough. Rhi needed distracting from this ridiculous business with Max and she knew just the guy for the job. She plucked Rhi's phone from where it was sticking out of Rhi's shirt pocket and pressed a couple of buttons.

"What are you doing?" Rhi said in alarm, trying to snatch her phone back.

Lila lifted the phone out of Rhi's reach, scrolling quickly through the names until she found the one she wanted. *Brody Baxter.*

"Yo, Rhi," said a familiar voice.

"Hi Brody – it's Lila."

Rhi gasped at Brody's name. "Lila, no!"

Lila pirouetted out of Rhi's way, giggling as Rhi made a vain snatch for the phone again. "Listen, Brody," she said, "are you busy tonight?"

"What are you suggesting?"

"I don't know if you heard, but the Heartbeat's reopening tonight and we need a headline act. Will you come over and sing with Rhi?"

"Sure," said Brody easily. "Rhi and I have been working on some new material that could use an audience. What time do you want me?"

"Eight?"

"You got it. See you then."

Rhi groaned and sank on to the stage with her head in her hands as Lila hung up. Polly grinned approvingly. Polly couldn't stand Max. Brody was the perfect solution.

"I can't believe you did that," Rhi muttered as Lila lobbed her phone back.

"Chill out, Rhi," Lila sighed. "Everyone knows how much you fancy Brody."

"We have a professional relationship," said Rhi. "Not a—"

"Physical one, we know," Polly put in. "Let's hope that changes tonight, shall we?"

"You two are impossible," Rhi complained.

"You love it really," said Lila, laughing.

Her phone buzzed.

Hey babe.
Meet me at 6 at the secret cove on the beach?
Kieran

Lila had no idea who Kieran was. Maybe it was the bartender she'd kissed at the last wedding reception they'd waitressed at. Then again, it could be half a dozen other guys. She'd been handing her number out like sweeties lately. She couldn't keep up.

"Who's it from?" asked Polly.

"Kieran," said Lila.

Rhi looked interested. "Who's Kieran?"

Something told Lila that her friends wouldn't be too impressed to learn about her confusion.

"A new friend," she said instead.

It was kind of exciting, now she thought about it. Meeting a mystery guy at the beach.

Is going alone to meet some random guy on the beach such a smart idea? said a small voice in her head, sounding very much like Polly. Lila ignored it.

Might see you there. Might not. . .

She giggled as she pressed 'send'. It was almost five o'clock. If she hurried home and got changed, she could make it to the beach AND get back to the Heartbeat in time for tonight's show.

What was the worst that could happen?

FOUR

The sun had disappeared behind the clouds as Lila walked along the beach with her hands thrust deep into the pockets of her favourite jacket. She felt nervous and excited and alive, and she treasured the feeling. It beat hollow misery any day.

Near the back of the Marine Parade Hotel, a sudden memory brought Lila up short. She'd almost met a secret admirer at the secret cove once before. She still had the anonymous notes she was given during her first difficult week at Heartside High. She even looked at them every now and again, late at night when Ryan's face wouldn't leave her alone. She had a pretty good idea who had sent them – Josh Taylor – but she had never been completely sure.

So much time had passed since then. So many dates and kisses and parties. Rivalry followed by friendship with Eve. Meeting Polly, dating Ollie and even stranger – Polly and Ollie getting together and Lila realizing she was actually fine with it. Then there had been arguments and drama and Rhi's close call with singing superstardom. The idea that Josh might still like her, after all this time, was highly unlikely. Besides, she had never fancied Josh. Not really. Not seriously.

Instead of meeting her secret admirer that night, she had run into Santiago, her ex-boyfriend from London instead. Lila's fingers went absently to the little tattoo on her wrist, following the curving lines of the ink. Even though she had since asked a tattooist to disguise them in the centre of the swirling heart, Lila knew that Santiago's initials were still there. How dumb she had been, getting them imprinted into her skin – like Santiago was going to be a permanent fixture in her life.

Back then I guess I did believe in The One, she thought. She was older and wiser now.

Ryan would never be older, or wiser.

Lila shivered as the usual feelings of guilt swirled through her. *Don't think about him*, she told herself. But it was impossible. The questions nagged at her brain, round and round. How could he be here one minute and then gone for ever? She didn't understand. You studied and worked hard and tried to do the right thing, but what did it matter?

You're here to meet Kieran, she reminded herself. *Not dwell on Ryan.*

The beach was empty except for the screaming gulls. Lila walked down to the water's edge and followed the frilling waves towards the path that led to the secret cove. The familiar rocky outline of Kissing Island sat on the horizon, its sandy causeway covered by the incoming sea.

When she had first heard the popular Heartside Bay legend about Kissing Island, Lila had found it irresistibly romantic.

"*You can only walk to it when the tides are just right. . . If you kiss your true love on Kissing Island at midnight of a full moon, you will be together forever.*"

That's what Polly had told her, the first time they came to the beach together. It was a lovely dream, but she didn't believe in true love any more. Far better to live in the moment.

Nothing lasts for ever, she thought.

As she approached the end of Marine Parade with its tall white clock tower, she spotted a familiar figure sitting on the sea wall. It was Josh, drawing like always, looking out at the curling waves and then down again at his sketchbook.

For some reason Lila felt annoyed at seeing him there. Josh had been the first one to reach Ryan's body in the sea on that hideous night, but he seemed totally cool about it. He was so smart and serious, doing as well as ever at school, drawing his pictures and just basically being Josh.

How could anyone hold it together after something like that? Lila wondered irritably. It wasn't natural. Josh needed to loosen up, show his sensitive side.

She waved at him to get his attention.

"Hey loser," she quipped. "Drawing boring seagulls again?"

Looking up, Josh shut his sketch pad abruptly. There was a strange, awkward silence that Lila wasn't expecting.

"Cat got your tongue?" she enquired, setting her hands on her hips.

Josh got up and dusted down his trousers, sliding his sketch pad into his bag and pushing his glasses up his nose in the familiar gesture Lila had come to know. For some reason he wouldn't look at her.

Lila'd always thought she and Josh got on pretty well. But right now she felt awkward, like she'd interrupted something. It made her feel more irritated than ever.

"Don't I even get a hey back?" she said after a moment.

Josh shrugged. "Hey back," he said.

Give him the benefit of the doubt, Lila told herself. Perhaps he'd show her what he'd been drawing if she asked. He'd done some great sketches at the Funky Fox Festival, including one or two of her.

"Did I interrupt something interesting for a change?" she asked, trying to find her way into a conversation. "Did you see a seagull with three wings, maybe?"

But Josh was already walking away.

Nettled now, Lila gave chase.

"Josh, what's going on? Why won't you look at me?"

Josh glanced sideways at her, looking bored. "How's this?"

His weird attitude reminded Lila of when she'd first come to Heartside Bay. Suddenly she remembered why, back then, she'd thought he was the rudest boy she'd ever met.

"Are you angry with me?" she asked.

Josh seemed to be speeding up. "Why would I be angry with you?" he threw over his shoulder. "I'm not your dad. See you around."

Lila felt hurt. "What have I done?" she asked.

Josh's long stride had put some distance between them now. He didn't answer.

"Fine," she shouted after him, angry now as he broke into a gentle jog and disappeared into the High Street. "Be like that. See if I care."

Why had he treated her like that? Like she was a worthless piece of flotsam washed up on the beach, along with all the plastic bottles and old shoes and bits of string? Lila felt hot and angry all over. She'd thought Josh was her friend. It seemed that she was wrong.

Typical, she thought. *As if I haven't got enough problems already.*

The clock tower chimed six with a tinny sound above her head. Lila forced herself to stop churning over what had happened with Josh and focus on her mystery date instead. She'd been determined to have a good time tonight, and she was going to be late.

She jumped down on to the sand and hurried towards the path to the secret cove. Kieran would be waiting, whoever he was.

I have better things to think about than Josh Taylor, she thought angrily.

FIVE

Lila paused on the path. She was feeling a little breathless, a combination of nerves and walking too quickly, irritated by how rude Josh had been to her. Turning up to her mystery date gasping for breath wouldn't be a good look.

Feeling around in her pocket, she took out a little compact mirror and a tube of lip gloss. She studied her reflection carefully. Her eyes looked dark. She hadn't bothered to take her mascara off the night before, just layered on more today and hoped for the best. The smudgy result looked good, she decided.

She tousled her hair a little more. Then she pursed her lips and swiped them with a layer of pink lip gloss, smacking them together to spread the colour more evenly.

Kieran will probably kiss it off the moment we meet, she thought, taking a certain amount of pleasure in the thought. *Josh would definitely disapprove.*

The moment she thought of Josh, her mood darkened again. He had been so cold towards her. Why was he so unpredictable? It was infuriating.

Satisfied that she looked her best, she slid her mirror and lip gloss back into her pocket and sauntered on down the path. The sun had come out from the clouds and was turning the stone cliffs around her a bright and dazzling gold. It was beautiful. Sometimes it really was worth living by the sea.

The long-haired biker from the previous night was standing on the beach, gazing out to sea. Lila stopped, suddenly overwhelmed with disappointment. She wanted a distraction, not a repeat performance. Maybe it wasn't too late to go home. She started to turn round, stumbling on the stones.

The sound made him look round. To her horror, Lila realized he was holding a cheap bunch of flowers in his hand.

Great, Lila thought, feeling trapped. *Now what?*

She thought of her friends still hard at work at the

Heartbeat, preparing for tonight. More than anything she suddenly wished she was with them.

Kieran had reached her now. He swung her up in his arms, kissing her soundly on the lips. "Miss me?" he said, putting her down again and thrusting the flowers into her hand.

"It's only been a few hours," Lila said weakly.

Kieran waved his free arm at the beach. "Girls like romantic stuff like this," he said. "Flowers and all that. Hey, I brought a picnic."

He dragged Lila over to where a rug had been spread out on the sand.

"This is a picnic?" Lila said, staring at the two cans of soda, half-bar of chocolate and already opened packet of crisps.

"What can I say? You were late. I got hungry."

Kieran sat down on the rug, pulling Lila down with him. She stumbled and tipped awkwardly into his lap.

"I like a girl who's keen," he grinned.

Lila flushed and wriggled into a more comfortable position. She set the flowers down where she didn't have to look at them. They reminded her of the flowers outside the church at Ryan's funeral.

Don't think of Ryan.

The sand beneath the rug was damp. Kieran had laid it too close to the tideline. She could feel the salty wetness seeping into the knees of her jeans.

"Crisp?" He offered her the pack with a gust of cheese-and-onion breath.

"Not really my flavour," said Lila, trying not to wrinkle her nose.

Had she really fancied this guy last night? Now he looked greasy and uninteresting, particularly without his bike. It didn't help that her pink lip gloss had smeared on to his lips from when he'd kissed her.

Kieran tipped the crisps into his mouth then crumpled up the bag, tossed it over his shoulder and belched. "So, what do you want to do?" he said, pushing his long hair away from his face. "We could take another ride. The bike's parked up on the coast road. I know a great place inland, where the views are awesome. Or maybe a movie? I—"

"Kieran, please stop."

He stopped, and looked at her. His eyes were smaller than she remembered.

"What?" he said. "You don't like movies?"

This was horribly awkward. But Lila had to say something.

"It's not that," she began.

He frowned. "You don't like bikes?"

This was so embarrassing. Lila forced herself to look him in the eye.

"Listen, Kieran. This is all very nice and everything, but . . . I'm not looking for a boyfriend."

He looked surprised. "You're not? But you seemed really keen last night."

Lila flushed a little. "I was just looking for some fun," she said. "I'm sure you're a really nice guy and everything, but I'm not interested in a relationship."

The silly smile had dropped off his face now.

"But I really like you," he said, looking hurt. "I thought you felt the same."

Why can't he get the message without me having to spell it out? Lila thought.

"You don't even know me," she said patiently.

He caught her hand and held it tightly against his chest. "I was looking forward to *getting* to know you," he said. "Can't you even give me a chance?"

Lila found herself getting irritated now. This was

so stupid. They'd only shared a few kisses and a motorcycle ride, for goodness sake. This guy was acting like something out of *Romeo and Juliet*.

"Please." Kieran was squeezing Lila's hand so tightly her finger bones were starting to hurt. "A chance is all I'm asking for?"

Lila had a horrible feeling that he was going to start crying. How had this got so out of hand? She tried to pull away from his grip, but he wouldn't let go.

"I'm sorry, Kieran," she said, tugging helplessly. "I didn't mean to hurt you. I thought you understood that it was just a one-off thing."

"You gave me your number," he pointed out.

"I know, but I didn't think you'd use it!"

His eyes were turning cold now. "That's generally what phone numbers are for."

"I really am sorry," Lila repeated. She couldn't keep tugging her hand away – it was getting seriously awkward now. "You're a great guy and I'm sure there's a really nice girl out there for you somewhere. We can just be friends, can't we?"

She leaned across and tried to kiss him on the cheek.

Instantly he turned his head and pressed his lips against hers. They were sticky and strawberry-flavoured.

"No," Lila said, pulling back at once.

"Can't you see how great we'd be together?" he said, trying to pull her back towards him again.

"No!" Lila was starting to panic now. He was stronger than she was.

"I really like you," he insisted, trying to kiss her again. "Let me show you how much I like you."

Fear was starting to stroke cold fingers down Lila's spine now. They were alone on a secret beach, far away from prying eyes.

"Let me GO!" she screamed.

SIX

Lila felt Kieran's grip loosening. She wrenched away from him, falling back into the sand with a thud, breathing heavily, her heart racing like a greyhound on a track.

Kieran was struggling to his feet to confront whoever had interrupted them. From her position on the sand, Lila looked up at the tall figure above her, all the way to the familiar face at the top.

Josh's face was set like granite. "She *said* no," he said. "Didn't you hear her?"

"This is none of your business, mate," said Kieran angrily. There was sand in his long dark hair. "My girlfriend—"

"She's not your girlfriend, and you know it."

Josh held out a hand to Lila without looking at her. Lila grabbed it and pulled herself to her feet. She was shivering.

"Who do you think you are?" Kieran blustered. He came towards Lila again. Lila cringed back.

"Lila's guardian angel," Josh said. "If you must know."

Kieran threw himself at Josh. Lila screamed as Josh sank a punch into Kieran's belly that sent the biker sprawling on to the sand again.

"Man, that hurt," said Josh under his breath, shaking out his fist.

Lila didn't know whether to laugh or cry. She stayed where she was, tucked safely behind Josh. She didn't think her legs would move even if she asked them.

Kieran was clutching his belly and groaning. He stumbled to his feet. "This isn't over," he wheezed.

"Oh yes it is," said Josh conversationally. "You just assaulted the daughter of Heartside Bay's Chief of Police. You're going to have lots of fun down at the station explaining that one."

Kieran paled. "I like her," he whined.

Josh snorted. "Funny way of showing it. Shove off, mate. She's not interested. And learn a few manners while you're at it."

Kieran gave Lila a last imploring look, but Lila stared at the sand. She didn't look up until she heard him swearing and walking away up the path towards the cliff road, leaving nothing but silence and the swish of the sea behind him.

Lila threw her arms around Josh's neck and held him tightly against her. Tears were flowing uncontrollably down her face. How had she got herself into such a stupid situation? How had she become this person? She hadn't meant for any of this to happen.

"Shh," said Josh, holding her gently. "It's OK. The Greaseball has gone."

Lila giggled, then started crying again. "Thank you," she mumbled into Josh's shoulder.

"No problem. I beat up bikers every day."

Lila was grateful that Josh wasn't telling her off. She was so sick of being in trouble all the time. It felt really good just to feel his arms around her while she cried herself stupid.

"Your taste in men stinks," he said over her head.

"I know," Lila hiccupped, burrowing a little closer. "But he did have a really great bike."

She felt Josh laugh against her hair. He smelled warm and lovely, and the nubby wool of his jumper felt cosy against her tear-streaked cheeks. Lila felt as if she could stay like this for ever. With Josh's arms round her, even thoughts of Ryan receded. She felt safe and calm for the first time in weeks.

When she felt sufficiently in control of herself, she pulled back to look into his lovely familiar face.

"How did you know I was here?" she asked, feeling strangely shy.

"Guardian angels know everything," said Josh.

Lila whacked him on the shoulder. "Seriously. How did you know?"

"I followed you. You had this wild look in your eye when you came up to me by the clock tower, like you were about to do something stupid. You've been doing a lot of that lately," he added dryly.

Lila winced. Josh was right.

"I didn't want to be a part of it," he continued. "But then I got worried and came back to the beach. Your footprints were easy enough to follow."

She had acted a bit intense now she came to think of it. She remembered how much Josh hated drama. "Sorry about the boring seagull thing," she said, colouring a little. "I didn't mean it. You draw beautiful seagulls."

"Even ones with just two wings?" Josh enquired.

Lila giggled. "Even those."

Josh still had his arms round her. Their faces were very close. Suddenly, overwhelmingly, Lila wanted to kiss him.

Fire flickered through her veins at the thought of Josh's mouth on hers. At that precise moment, Lila had never wanted anything so much in her life. He would complete her. He would make all the bad stuff go away. It would be just him and her, kissing.

Everything seemed to go into slow motion as the thought went through her mind. And with a jolt like lightning, she understood that he was thinking it too.

They stared at each other. No one was laughing any more. Josh's lips were so close. If she just stood on tiptoe, she would feel them on her own. His arms tightened around her back. He was dipping his head towards hers, his eyes closing. They were moments away from. . .

From what?

Heartbreak.

Lila pulled back. Blood was thundering through her head, confusing her. She couldn't do this. Not to Josh. Not now, when she felt so lost. He had saved her, but she wouldn't confuse gratitude with . . . anything else. She would only hurt him like she hurt every guy she came close to. Like she had hurt Ryan. The thought of hurting Josh, dear lovely Josh, was unbearable.

If she kissed him, she wouldn't be able to walk away like she'd done with so many other guys. Josh was different. He was too important to mess around with.

She swerved to the side and planted an awkward kiss on his cheek.

"Thanks," she said, pushing him firmly away. She gave him a friendly pat on the shoulder, like he was a dog. "For everything, Josh. I mean it."

He looked so confused that it almost broke her heart. Then she turned round and ran towards the path that led back to the main beach, the town and sanity.

SEVEN

"Earth to Lila?"

Lila stopped chewing her nails and focused. "What?"

Polly was looking at her with a puzzled frown. "Are you OK?"

Lila didn't know where to begin. "Not really," she said, deciding to keep it simple. "But don't worry, I'll be fine."

"If you're sure," Polly said doubtfully.

Lila pulled herself together. She had been so busy watching the Heartbeat Café door for Josh that she had completely missed Rhi and Brody's first two songs. There was still no sign of him, thankfully.

Lila still wasn't quite sure what had happened

between them at the secret cove. But she knew she didn't want to face Josh again just yet.

"It's so good to see the Heartbeat coming back to life, isn't it?" she said as Rhi and Brody retuned their guitars and consulted about their next song. She looked around at the crowds of people near the bar and by the stage.

"It's brilliant," Polly agreed. "I know I didn't want Rhi contacting Max about the social media thing, but I'm really glad she did."

"He's built the new website already?" said Lila in surprise.

Polly shook her head. "That'll take him a week or two. This lot are here because he basically invited everyone he knows on Facebook."

Max and Ollie were sitting opposite them, laughing about something. Lila still didn't trust Max. She didn't like the way he was smiling at Rhi on the stage either. She really hoped he hadn't snared Rhi in his net all over again. Rhi was way too nice for Max.

"Thanks for your patience," said Brody into the mic. "We have a love song for you now called 'Sweet Summer'."

The beat was gentle and swaying, the words full of love and promise. One or two people got up from the tables to dance.

"Come on," said Ollie, reaching over the table for Polly's hand. "I want to show you off."

They were very cute together, Lila acknowledged, if a little unexpected. Never in a million years would she have put little, intellectual Polly with tall, football-loving Ollie. But they worked somehow. They looked happy, dancing with their arms round each other.

Love does strange things to people, she thought.

It was weird to think that she and Ollie had danced like that once.

Her fingers went to the tattoo on her wrist, like they often did when she thought about love. She realized she felt jealous of what Ollie and Polly had. It wasn't that she wanted to go out with Ollie again, but still . . . it felt strange. She'd always struggled to stay friends with guys she'd dated. For Polly's sake, in this case she really had to try.

Lila glanced at the door again, in case Josh had appeared in the last five minutes. Turning back to her soda, she caught the eye of Rhi's dad behind the bar.

Or, to be more accurate, she caught sight of his hand waving at her over the top of the pressing crowd.

Pushing her drink to one side, she headed over. "Need some help, Mr Wills?"

"That would be great," said Rhi's dad. "I need some more glasses from the back room. Could you fetch them for me?"

Lila was happy for something to do. It might stop her thinking about Josh. "Sure," she said. "Where's the back room?"

"Behind the stage." He pointed at a door. "Go that way, it's quicker than round by the kitchens."

There was a burst of applause as Lila made her way across the café towards the door Mr Wills had indicated.

"Thanks," Brody said into the mic. "We're going to take a short break now. Back in five."

The door was a little stiff, but Lila managed to force it open with her shoulder. She followed a short, dark corridor around the back of the stage to a cold room full of glasses and cleaning products. As she was grabbing a crate of glasses, she overheard Brody's voice through the curtain behind her.

"Guess what? I've fixed us three more gigs."

"Seriously?" said Rhi. She sounded delighted.

Lila could hear the smile in Brody's voice. "Never more so. They'll even pay us. I think it's beginning, Rhi."

Rhi clapped her hands. "That's awesome! *You* are awesome, Brody!" Something made Lila glance up at the silence that followed. Through a chink in the curtain dividing the back room from the backstage area, she saw Rhi and Brody had clunked together in an awkward, half-hug, half-kiss. It looked as if Rhi had been aiming for Brody's cheek, while Brody'd had different ideas.

Lila heard Rhi laugh with embarrassment. "Whoa, sorry. Awkward."

"Not for me." Brody's reply was soft and certain.

Lila knew she was intruding. She reversed swiftly towards the corridor that would take her back to the bar. She would pretend she hadn't heard or seen a thing.

The curtain ripped open as Rhi rushed into the back room, almost crashing into Lila.

"Hey," said Lila, startled and staggering. The

51

glasses clinked ominously as she struggled not to drop them.

"Lila, sorry!" Rhi gasped. "I didn't know you were back here. Are you OK?" She stopped, adding in a low voice, "Did you see what just happened with Brody? I'll help you with those if you want. Did Dad ask you to fetch them?"

Lila could feel herself blushing. "Pretend I wasn't there, Rhi," she said, squirming.

"No, no, it's fine." Rhi looked a little feverish. "I think Brody was going to kiss me. Do you think he was going to kiss me?"

"Did you want him to kiss you?"

Rhi bit her lip. "I don't know," she confessed. She led the way back down the corridor towards the main room, the glasses clinking in her hands. "There was this . . . magic in the air, almost, when I thought he was going to do it. He's an amazing guy, Lila. But I don't want to mess up our relationship. We sing together. He's got us more gigs. Getting involved with him could mess everything up. I don't want to risk that. I should keep my music and my love life separate, right?"

The glasses were heavy. Lila shifted them into a

more comfortable position as Rhi pushed open the door to a blast of chatter. "I'm hardly the person to ask," she said, threading through the crowd behind Rhi. "But if you really want my opinion, you're taking this way too seriously. You like him and he likes you. You want to kiss each other. Simple."

Lila saw how Rhi's eyes flitted to Max, leaning lazily back in his chair and chatting to Ollie. "It's not simple at all," she sighed.

Josh's confused face swam into Lila's mind. She pushed it away. She wished all these thoughts of Ryan and Josh would leave her alone. *Why be serious about any guy at all?* she asked herself. *Life is short. It should be about fun, not feelings.*

She plonked the glasses on the bar, feeling irritable. Glancing around the room, her eyes settled on a table of boys wearing hoodies from the local university at the back of the room. One of them caught her eye and smiled.

Relief swamped Lila. The perfect distraction.

"Look at those lovely boys over there," she said, nudging Rhi. "I'm going over to make friends."

Rhi frowned. "Take care, Lila."

Take care, take care. . . Was that all anyone said around here? Lila had a sudden flash memory of the fear she had felt with Kieran a few hours earlier. Her thoughts careered instantly to Josh. How he had rescued her. How he'd sent Biker Boy packing, and held her, and how warm and safe he smelled. How they had almost—

Fire stirred in her belly again, together with some unpleasant butterflies. Now she *definitely* needed distracting.

"I can look after myself, Rhi," she said, tousling her hair and shooting flirtatious glances at the uni table. She was rewarded by one guy raising his coffee at her. "I'll see you later. Remember what I said, OK? Keep it simple."

And she made her way through the crowd to have some fun.

EIGHT

Robbie's hand felt warm in hers as Lila dragged him up the Heartbeat Café's old twisting staircase towards the roof garden.

"You *have* to see the best view in Heartside," she said, glancing over her shoulder at him. "It's totally worth the climb."

"I have a pretty good view already, thanks," he said, grinning up at her.

He was tall and blond, with sleepy green eyes and a nicely fitted T-shirt. Lila couldn't wait to put her arms round him and feel his muscles under her fingers. The roof garden would be perfect for a little fun and flirtation.

She'd been spoiled for choice on the uni boys' table.

At least three of them had been cute, and she'd enjoyed herself hugely as she watched them competing for her attention. Robbie had been the winner, with a dry humour that had tickled her. It was time for his – and her – reward.

As they made it to the top landing, Lila's hand hesitated on the door. It was Robbie, right? Or was this Nick? She tried to remember. There had been so many names. . .

Robbie/Nick came up close behind her and dropped a kiss just below her ear. Lila's insides melted. She reached behind her and caressed his head. The hair on the nape of his neck felt soft and bristly.

Does it matter what his name is? she thought. *He's hot and that's all that counts.*

The terrace was large, and well planted with pots and a pretty trellis that was creeping with vines and flowers. There were benches dotted around, and the sound of water from a little water feature in the corner. The town glittered below them, a sweep of orange street lights that ended abruptly at the great blackness of the ocean.

Nick/Robbie whistled. "I see what you mean," he

said, dropping her hand and leaning over the wall to gaze at the view. "I can't believe I've never been here before."

Lila selected her favourite bench, tucked into a corner near the water feature. She slid her hand into his, tugging him with her. "So Robbie," she said, hoping it wasn't Nick. "Has anyone told you lately how completely lovely you are?"

"It's Luke," he said, looking a little surprised.

Lila was glad the lights up here were dim. She was blushing like a fire engine. "I meant Luke, sorry," she fudged. "I was so lost in your big green eyes that my brain just imploded."

It sounded cheesy, but Luke seemed to like it. He grinned suddenly. "You're very unexpected," he said, brushing a strand of hair away from her face. "I don't know what you'll say next. You don't strike me as a small-town girl, Lila. Have you lived in Heartside Bay long?"

"Long enough to know what I like about it," she said, hoping he'd get the hint.

He turned back to the view again. "How far can you see up here?"

"About a metre," Lila said, running her hands up the front of his T-shirt.

He peeled her hands away, laughing. "Direct, aren't you? There's plenty of time for that later. Tell me more about yourself."

Great. A talker. Like she didn't have enough talkers in her life already. *Kiss me already*, she thought impatiently.

"I'm fifteen and bored," she said. Then, because it was clearly expected of her, "You?"

"Nineteen tomorrow," he said, still staring at the view. "And I'm not bored at all."

"You think this is exciting?" Lila said, sliding her hands up the front of his T-shirt again. "You've seen nothing yet, birthday boy."

It was clear that she was going to have to do all the work here. Reaching for the back of his neck, she pulled him towards her for a kiss. He froze in surprise, then kissed her back. His mouth was soft and a little hesitant.

Josh would probably be hesitant too, Lila thought, pulling Luke closer, encouraging him. *To begin with, at least.* She imagined Josh's tall, lean body in her arms, his arms around her back just as he'd held her that afternoon at the beach. She dreamily brushed against his lips, meeting his gentleness with some of her own.

Except she wasn't kissing Josh. She was kissing Luke.

Lila tried to put herself back into the moment, pulling Luke more tightly towards her, but the image of Josh's mouth on hers had unsettled her.

"Whoa," said Luke as he came up for air. "You're hungry, aren't you? Not to mention adorable."

Lila felt the usual rush of disappointment. The first kiss was always the best one. Now there would just be more of the same. She wished she could turn the clock back, to that moment when she had first pulled Luke towards her. But time was annoying like that. You could never recapture the moment.

They weren't alone, she realized. Behind Luke she could see another couple in the shadows, wrapped in each other's arms. That cloud of dark hair was instantly recognizable. Lila smiled to herself.

Looks like Rhi took my advice after all, she thought, pleased for her friend.

Something wasn't right with the picture though. The boy Rhi was kissing wasn't straw-blond like Brody. He was dark, with almost as much hair as Rhi.

Lila wanted to groan with frustration.

Rhi was snogging Max.

What does she see in him? she wondered. *He's a two-timing toad!* Max would only break Rhi's heart all over again.

Luke kissed her again. Lila tried to respond with the same level of enthusiasm. He pushed her hair away from her face and cupped her chin with one hand. "When can I see you again?" he said.

"You want to see me again?" she said a little stupidly. Her head was still spinning over the Rhi/Max thing.

"Sure," he said in surprise. "You're cute and funny and you kiss like a superstar. What's not to like?"

Lila felt the old dread creeping over her. She extricated herself from his arms, backing away a little. "That's really nice of you, Luke, but I kind of have a regular boyfriend," she lied.

"Clearly he isn't very nice to you, or you wouldn't

be kissing me," Luke replied, reaching for her hand again.

"Sorry," Lila said, shaking her head. "I don't think we can see each other again. Anyway, you go back to uni tomorrow, don't you?"

He looked puzzled, and a little hurt. "So? It's not that far away. I can come to Heartside any time. I want to spend more time with you, Lila."

The look in his eyes reminded her of Ryan. That puppy-dog look that had made her laugh. She had never felt the same way about him, but he'd still followed her around, hoping for her attention. He'd even chartered a boat, specially to come to Eve's party and surprise her with a romantic declaration on the beach. She'd rewarded him for that with a kiss, and look where it had got him.

"Are you stupid or something?" she said abruptly. "I don't *want* to go out with you. Find someone nicer. I'm not worth your time, Luke."

She walked quickly towards the roof-garden door that would lead back to the bar. Once again, she was crushing the hope out of a boy. Ryan. Kieran. Josh. Now Luke.

Why did she keep hurting people? She didn't mean to. She was cursed.

She had to get out of the Heartbeat before she started crying.

NINE

Tears blurred Lila's eyes as she half-walked, half-ran through the bar. People were turning to look at her, but she was past caring.

"What's the rush, darling?"

Lila looked a little blurrily into a pair of perfectly made-up grey eyes.

"Eve?" she said, trying to focus. "When did you get here?"

"Too late, clearly," said Eve, folding her arms. She was looking immaculate as usual, her glossy auburn hair bouncing on her blue cashmere-clad shoulders like a shampoo ad. "What's the matter?"

Lila had a horrible feeling Luke would be following her down the stairs at any moment, making embarrassing declarations. She grabbed Eve's arm. "Can we get out of here?" she begged. "I need some air."

"This sounds exciting," said Eve, letting Lila lead her out of the doors. "Today has been so dreadfully dull, I could use a little distraction. Tell auntie Eve all about it."

The air was cool and clear outside the café. Lila towed Eve through the cobbled lanes of the Old Town to the beach.

"How romantic," Eve said, looking around her at the empty sweep of beach. "Are you going to tell me you love me?"

Eve could always make Lila laugh, even at moments as traumatic as these.

"In your dreams," she returned, grinning.

They'd come a long way since clashing over Ollie, way back in the distant past. Once she would have happily thrown Eve into the sea that whispered and curled along the shore in front of her. Now Eve was just the person she needed to talk to.

"Why do boys always want more?" she asked.

Eve settled herself on the sea wall, brushing a

little gingerly at the seaweed that clung to the bricks. "You're asking the wrong person, darling," she said. "I like girls, remember?"

Lila was hardly likely to forget. Eve's sexuality had been a source of school gossip for weeks now. Lila and the others had rallied around, and people were finally starting to get used to the idea. Eve hadn't found a girlfriend yet, but Lila had a feeling that it wouldn't take long.

"You're not the wrong person," Lila said firmly. "You are entirely the right person. You used to complain about never feeling anything for the boys you dated, remember? You practically used to boast about breaking their hearts."

"Poor things," said Eve. "You're right, of course. Then again, I'm irresistible."

"Be serious for a moment, will you?" Lila begged. She sat down beside Eve on the sea wall. She had to talk about this or she would go mad. "Why can't boys just take what I'm offering? Fun and no complications?"

Eve tapped her dark-blue painted nails on the sleeves of her cardigan. "Who wants more?"

"Everyone," Lila said gloomily.

"Get you," said Eve, with a flash of the waspishness that had made her so terrifying to Lila in the early days. "Lady Popular."

"I think maybe I'm cursed," Lila groaned, too miserable to defend herself from Eve's mocking remark. "First Ryan, then this Kieran guy on a motorcycle that I met a few days ago, then. . ." She had been going to say *Josh*. Something stopped her.

"Then who?" Eve asked. "A guy in the Heartbeat? Someone I know?"

Lila shook her head. "He was called Luke," she said wearily. "He's not local. I'm not cut out for dating, Eve. You could ask Ryan about that, except. . ."

"Except he's dead," said Eve bluntly. "Lila, you can't blame yourself if you don't feel anything for these boys."

Lila felt the tears welling up. "Ryan wanted so much from me," she said, wiping her eyes with the sleeve of her jacket. "And I couldn't give it to him. He had to show off to prove how interesting he was, like somehow the scales would fall from my eyes and I would suddenly like him as much as he liked me." She swallowed. "He jumped off that cliff because of me."

"He jumped off that cliff because he was an idiot," said Eve. "I don't like to speak ill of the dead, but that's the truth."

Lila groaned, clutching at her hair. "Why is everything so serious?" she said. "Why can't life be more *fun*?"

Eve's eyes gleamed in the streetlight over their heads. "Darling, you've just given me a tremendous idea. We need fun. Both of us. The only thing anyone seems to do in this town is fall in love. I can hardly move for the gloom. Let's go to London tomorrow."

"London?" Lila repeated.

Eve had jumped off the sea wall. "My treat. We could go on the London Eye maybe, and have a fabulous lunch somewhere with a view. And of course, take in some retail therapy."

"Topshop on Oxford Circus?" said Lila, interested now.

Eve pulled a face. "Darling, please. Knightsbridge only. What do you say?"

Lila was seriously tempted. "I don't think my parents will let me go to London," she said weakly. "They aren't too pleased with me at the moment."

"Honestly, Lila," said Eve, "I thought you had more backbone than that. Ask them. Beg, plead. It works for me every time."

"You're right," said Lila. She pictured the hustle and bustle of London – the shops, the crowds, the cafés, the sights. In London she wouldn't have a moment to think about all the bad stuff. It was just what she needed. She hugged Eve impulsively. "I'll talk to them tonight."

"That's more like it," said Eve. "Talk to them and call me as soon as you have their permission. I have to plan my wardrobe, which will take until midnight at the very least."

Lila hurried home, her mind sparking with thoughts of a day in London with Eve and her gold credit card. She checked the time on her phone. It was only nine-thirty. She would get a few brownie points for getting home early, wouldn't she? It might even help to persuade her parents that she deserved a day in London.

Her parents were sitting at the kitchen table when Lila burst into the house.

"Hi," she said breathlessly. She kissed her mother, and gave her father a squeeze. "Everyone OK?"

"Fine," said her mother, looking a little startled. "How was your evening?"

"Good," said Lila, doing her best to forget about what a disaster it had really been. "I wanted to ask you both a favour."

Her father folded his arms. "Here we go," he sighed.

Lila sat down beside him and took his hand. "Dad, I'm really sorry I was so horrible to you the other night," she said.

Her father gave a weary smile. "What are you after, Lila?"

"Can I go to London tomorrow with Eve?"

The strangest expression slid across her father's face. "Eve Somerstown?" he said.

"I don't know anyone else called Eve, Dad," said Lila, doing her best not to roll her eyes. "It's the holidays, and I'm starting with this tutor guy on Monday. I need a little break before all the hard work begins. Eve's invited me to London with her. She'll pay for everything."

"Over my dead body," said her father, sitting up suddenly.

Lila frowned. Why was her dad acting so weirdly about this? Eve was Heartside royalty. Her father was mayor of the town, for goodness sake. "That's a bit heavy, Dad," she said. "What's Eve ever done to you?" A horrible thought struck her. "Is it because she's gay?"

"Of course not. For goodness sake, Lila, what kind of monster do you think I am?" her father protested, colouring. "I just mean . . . I don't think you should expect Eve to pay for you in London."

Lila pounced. "So I can go?"

"Let her, Greg," Lila's mother said unexpectedly. "Lila's right, she does have the tutor starting on Monday. She can have a little time off, can't she?"

Lila felt close to tears. She needed this. Her dad couldn't stop her going, could he? "We won't get into trouble, I promise," she said. "We're just going to do a little shopping and come home again. I'll take my own money if that really bothers you. I'll love you for ever if you let me go, Dad."

"I thought that was the deal anyway," he replied a little drily.

Lila made her eyes as wide and beseeching as she could. "Please?"

Her father looked like he was wrestling with something.

"You can go," he said at last. "But if there is one whisper of trouble, Lila, I will ground you until you're twenty-five."

"It's a deal," said Lila joyfully, and hugged both her parents hard.

A day in London was just a few hours away. She couldn't *wait*.

TEN

Lila stood on the banks of the river Thames and breathed in the familiar smell of the boats and the water. There were people everywhere. Busy market stalls lined the South Bank selling everything from soap to sausages, and the pavements were crowded with couples strolling hand in hand, small children holding balloons, well-dressed older ladies walking regally along and brightly dressed street artists. Amid the cacophony of chatter, the hooting of the boats and the music of the buskers, the great white wheel of the London Eye turned high above her head.

They had arrived at London Waterloo on an early train, and had already enjoyed a coffee at the British Film Institute beside Waterloo Bridge. Browsing the market stalls had taken a further hour, and Lila was laden with goodies: bright Indian bangles, a skull-and-crossbones scarf, a little backpack with a pug dog on the back.

Eve tapped Lila on the shoulder. "Our turn now," she said as a London Eye guide ushered them towards the slowly turning pods.

The views were all the more amazing for being revealed bit by bit as the wheel made its great 360-degree turn. Lila leaned on the rail and lost herself in the spectacle unfolding beneath her. The Houses of Parliament, the Shard, the winding silver ribbon of the river far below.

"I wonder if we can see Heartside Bay?" she said with a giggle.

"Forget that boring little place," said Eve. "We're in London now. Are you getting hungry? We'll go to Daddy's club for lunch."

Lila giggled as she pictured Eve's dad dancing around in a basement full of swirling dry ice. It was a funny image.

"You're so unsophisticated," Eve sighed, dragging Lila towards a long black taxi rank. "Watch and learn, grasshopper."

Lila hadn't ridden in many London taxis. The Tube was more her budget. She decided she liked it, with its spacious cab and comfy seats.

"Where is this club anyway?" she asked.

"Pall Mall. All the best clubs are in that area. Daddy's club does the most divine lobster," said Eve, leaning back against the leather seats.

Lila hoped she wouldn't have to choose a live lobster for the chef to boil, like they seemed to do on TV.

"Do they do steak?" she checked.

"Of course," said Eve. "The chef is French. Just don't ask for egg and chips. I hear he throws people out for that."

Lila enjoyed the sight of London whizzing past the taxi windows. In no time at all they had pulled up outside a large white building whose high oak door boasted the biggest brass door knocker she'd ever seen. A doorman in a tall black hat opened the doors for them as they went inside.

The entrance hall had a high, plastered ceiling and a large cream-coloured front desk. The marble busts that lined the walls seemed to be looking down on Lila with disapproval.

"Miss Somerstown?" said the rather stiff-looking man standing behind the desk. He looked surprised.

"We've come for lunch, James," said Eve. "You can put it on Daddy's account."

The manager looked uncomfortable. "Forgive my surprise just now, Miss Somerstown," he said, "but I wasn't expecting to see you here again. You see, your father is no longer a member of this club."

Eve laughed in astonishment. "What do you mean? Daddy's been a member here for fifteen years!"

"I don't dispute that, Miss Somerstown, but I'm afraid his membership lapsed some time ago. In fact. . ." he checked his computer screen, "it has been four months since he last paid his dues."

Lila had never seen Eve speechless before.

"Four months and fifteen days, to be precise," the manager added.

"It's a mistake," said Eve, recovering. "It must be."

The manager spread his hands apologetically. "I'm sorry, but there's nothing I can do."

The black-hatted doorman stepped towards them, preparing to usher them out of the door.

"I'm so embarrassed," Eve said as they stepped

outside into the sunshine again. "Why don't I call Daddy? I'm sure he'll clear up the mistake in no time."

"Don't," said Lila hastily, seeing an opportunity. "It was a bit stuffy in there anyway. Let's go somewhere more fun."

"I know!" said Eve, brightening up again. "There's a brilliant new restaurant called Velveteen on the river. It opened a couple of months ago to rave reviews. I'll call Caitlin to see if she can get us a table. Caitlin can *always* get tables."

Sure enough, Eve's friend Caitlin, who was a party planner and always seemed to have a connection of some sort, got them a table.

"It's a window table, so we'll be able to see the envy on everyone's faces as they walk past," Eve said happily as she pocketed her phone. "Now, we can't *possibly* go to lunch at Velveteen in what we're wearing. It's an extremely upmarket restaurant. We'll have to go to Bond Street right now and find something new."

Lila looked down at the flowered skirt and grey leggings she was wearing. "If this was good enough for your dad's club, I'm sure it'll be fine for this Velveteen place."

"Absolutely not," said Eve firmly. "We're talking about *first impressions* here, Lila. I won't have Velveteen's first impression of me in an outfit I've been wearing for nearly six hours already. The table's booked for two-thirty, so we have plenty of time to find exactly the right thing. Taxi!"

I could get used to this, Lila thought, leaning back in the comfy taxi as London streamed past the window once again. She wondered what it must be like to have gold credit cards and bags of confidence. This was the closest she'd ever get to understanding the glamorous life Eve led. There were butterflies of excitement in her belly as she thought about the famous shops on Bond Street. Armani, Burberry, Prada. . . For one brief moment she felt uneasy about what her dad had said, about not letting Eve pay for everything. If they were going shopping in some of London's most expensive boutiques, she wouldn't be able to buy a thing without Eve's help.

The first shop they went into had just one item in the window: a pale blue quilted handbag with a gold handle. *Probably real gold*, Lila thought, feeling a little dazzled.

"Can I help you?"

Lila swung round from contemplating the handbag.

"We're just looking, thanks," she said.

The very tall, very thin shop assistant flicked her eyes up and down Lila's grey leggings. "I think you and your friend would be happier in some of the stores on another street."

Lila felt annoyed by the girl's tone of voice. "We're quite happy as we are, thanks," she said. "How much is that dress?"

She pointed defiantly at a pretty pastel green dress on a golden mannequin.

The shop girl folded her arms. "At least a year's pocket money," she said. "As I say, you and your friend will be much happier in another shop."

Lila had had enough. Who did this girl think she was?

"I think you're right," she said, giving the girl her dirtiest look. "Your clothes suck anyway. Come on Eve, we're leaving."

Eve swung round from the elegant white blazer she had been looking at. "We are? I thought I'd try this on."

"Right now," said Lila, taking Eve by the arm.

"What was that about?" Eve complained as they stood outside again.

Lila was feeling so annoyed, she could hardly speak. "That shop girl talked to me like I was dirt," she said furiously. "She thought we couldn't afford to buy anything in there."

Eve clicked her teeth. "These girls work on commission, you know. We'll just have to spend twice as much money in the shop across the road instead, won't we? But first we need a blow-dry. Come on."

Eve pushed Lila into a chic hair salon a little way up the street for a proper blow-dry. Within twenty minutes, Lila's wild brown hair had changed into something unrecognizably sleek and shiny.

"*Now* we can go shopping," said Eve, checking her glossy reflection in the salon window with satisfaction as they came out again half an hour later.

Lila couldn't help feeling incredibly excited as Eve led her over the road, into a glamorous-looking store directly across the road from the snobby shop girl. These windows were much friendlier-looking, filled with the prettiest coats and jackets Lila had ever seen.

"Try this," said Eve, walking straight towards a rack filled with gorgeous colourful dresses. "The blue will look fantastic with your eyes. I'm going to try on that dark green jacket. The gold buttons are simply delicious."

Forty minutes later, Lila emerged from the shop with two bags in each hand. She was feeling more than a little dazed, and not at all like her usual slightly scruffy self. The short blue shimmery shift dress Eve had chosen for her was utterly gorgeous, flattering her long legs and her skin tone. With her glossy hair and new shoes on her feet, she looked and felt a million dollars.

Eve adjusted the front of her new primrose-yellow blazer, and flicked some imaginary dust off the pure white dress underneath. Her auburn hair sat as perfectly on her shoulders as ever, a fresh layer of make-up brightening her grey eyes and a new leaf-green handbag swinging by her side.

"Let's go and pay Lady Snooty a visit," she said with a nasty gleam in her eye.

Lila had never enjoyed walking into a shop more. The shop girl started towards them with a wide, welcoming smile on her face.

"Can I help you?"

"You tried that line already," said Lila. She swung her shopping bags off the ends of her fingers. "Too bad you missed out on all this lovely commission."

"You really ought to be nicer, you know," Eve added as the shop girl's face sagged with horrified recognition. "Manners don't cost a penny."

ELEVEN

"I'm having the best day," Lila sighed on the wide back seat of their latest taxi as it purred along the Embankment towards Velveteen. "Can we stay in London for ever?"

"You have tutoring tomorrow," Eve said, adjusting her gold watch strap. "Isn't that what you told me?"

Lila groaned. "Don't remind me. As Dad is fond of saying, 'We know what's best for you.' Blah blah blah. Like he knows anything about me! Have you noticed how patronizing people are towards teenagers? Lady Snooty is a perfect example. I'm so sick of being treated like a child."

"Let's not worry about real life just now," Eve advised. "We're two girls footloose in London, with plenty of money and two sensational outfits. We can be anyone we like."

Lila sat up. An idea was glimmering at the back of her mind. "Eve, you're a genius," she said in excitement. "We can be anyone, can't we? Let's choose new identities. Let's pretend to be other people for the rest of the day."

Eve considered this. "How about we tell the restaurant that we're the daughters of famous pop stars?" she suggested.

"I don't want to be anyone's daughter," Lila said at once. "I want to be treated as an adult for once. Let's say that we're reality TV stars or something."

"Over from America," Eve added, getting into the idea.

"Hello?" said Lila. "Our accents will give that away in two seconds!"

"OK, so we're British girls who ended up on a reality show in the States," said Eve. "A reality show about . . . about. . ."

"Fashion," Lila jumped in. "It will explain our outfits."

"Perfect," Eve said. "We've watched enough shows

like that to fake it like professionals. We're both tall enough to get away with the model thing. Don't you think?"

Lila gave Eve her best fashion pout. "Darling, we are totally the next big thing."

They spilled out of the taxi outside Velveteen, giggling madly. As Eve paid the cab driver, Lila threw back her shoulders and straightened her face. If they were going to get away with this, they had to get it exactly right.

Luckily, Eve was used to smart restaurants – even restaurants built entirely of gleaming glass, with huge pink flower arrangements and crystal, long-stemmed wine glasses and waiters in white jackets and breathtaking riverside views. Leaving their coats and shopping bags with the restaurant manager, they were ushered to their table at once.

"Wine, madam?" asked the waiter.

Lila wanted to laugh. If her parents could see her now. . .

"Goodness me, no," said Eve, settling down at the table. "Wine is terribly fattening, and we models have to watch our figures. We'll have two sparkling waters."

"Certainly. With or without our signature citrus twist?"

Two tall glasses filled with clear fizzing water, ice and three perfect curls of green, yellow and orange citrus rinds arrived at their table within moments. Lila let Eve order two large seafood salads for them to eat. She was too busy keeping her usual slouchy posture upright and model-like to say very much. One or two people were looking at them, leaning close to one another and whispering. It felt exhilarating, being here in these clothes, pretending to be someone other than boring Lila Murray from boring Heartside Bay.

"So far so good, Fifi," said Eve after the waiter had brought them their salads.

Lila almost snorted her fizzy water out of her nose. "Fifi? What kind of model name is that?"

"A completely brilliant one. I'm Lorelei, by the way." Eve tasted her salad and sighed with pleasure.

"Lorelei," Lila repeated. "I'll call you Lorry for short, shall I?"

They giggled their way through the meal, doing their best to remember to act like models. Lila knew models didn't generally eat pudding, but the sticky toffee sorbet looked and sounded so fantastic that she decided that she would try it.

"Armani won't cast you for his summer collection if you eat that, Fifi," said Eve, waving her coffee spoon under Lila's nose.

"Armani can jump in the river Thames, Lorry," Lila said, waving her sorbet spoon back. "This is way more important."

After Eve had paid the bill, they took a leisurely stroll along the river. The market stalls were still in full swing. Lila stopped at a stall, where a brooch shaped like a cat with rhinestone eyes had caught her eye.

"For you," she said, presenting Eve with the brooch. "Its eyes are real diamonds, of course."

Eve looked pleased. "You didn't have to buy that for me."

"There's no point earning good money on modelling shoots if I can't spend it on my mates," Lila said, grinning.

Eve pinned the cat brooch on her expensive yellow blazer. It glittered cheerfully in the afternoon sunshine.

"Who do you model with?"

A very tall, leggy girl with pixie-green eyes and a

large purple hat was standing at the hot dog stall next door. She had been listening to their conversation with a bright and interested look in her eye.

"Sorry if I sound nosy," she said. "I'm a model too, you see."

Lila scrabbled around for one of the lies they'd come up with over lunch. "An agency in the States," she said, shooting a helpless glance at Eve. "You won't have heard of it."

The girl grinned. "Try me. I modelled in the States last year."

Lila had a feeling their cover had just been blown. "Erm," she said, struggling to come up with a name.

"We were just messing around," Eve said, saving Lila's blushes. "We're not really models."

The purple-hatted girl laughed. "Glad to hear it. It's a very boring job. Standing around wearing weird things, prodded by stylists and blinded by camera flashes. Nice clothes, by the way."

Her name was Dee and she was on a shoot near the Tate Modern art gallery, not far from Velveteen. Lila couldn't quite believe they were talking to a real model.

"You could come along and watch if you like," Dee

offered, munching on her hot dog. "If you haven't got anything better to do. They're a cool crowd. We'll head along the river after the shoot for some fun. Why don't you join us?"

The rest of the afternoon passed in a haze of clothes, photographers, stylists, lighting assistants and two other models as tall and leggy as Dee. Lila and Eve were absorbed so easily into the group that it felt as if they'd known these people forever. Lila felt like she'd been given a glimpse into a secret world.

When the shoot was over, they followed Dee and the others along the river towards Tower Bridge and down into a huge cellar bar playing excellent music to an achingly hip crowd. Lila lost all track of time. She lost Eve as well, in the thick of the dancing crowd. It didn't matter. She was quite happy dancing with her new-found friends until she was breathless and gasping for a soda, watching the glamorous scene unfold around her.

Maybe I should be a model, she thought idly as she stood at the bar a couple of hours into the evening. Whatever Dee said, it looked like a fun life.

Lila wished she had a clearer idea of what she

wanted to be when she was older. Her friends seemed to be carving out paths for themselves already: Ollie and his football, Polly and her fashion, Max with his techie know-how and Rhi with her singing. All Lila had achieved so far was flunk a load of school tests which had landed her with a revision tutor for the rest of her holidays. It was a gloomy outlook.

"Whew," said Eve, arriving at the bar beside her. Her hair looked a little messier than usual, and beads of sweat glistened on her pale forehead. "What's the time?"

Lila checked her phone. The screen was ominously black.

"I'm out of power," she said. She squinted at the clock set high above the bottles at the bar. In the next moment she had shot out of her seat. "It's ten to eleven, Eve!" she gasped. "Our last train leaves in ten minutes!"

There wasn't even time to say goodbye to Dee and the others. Eve and Lila pelted out of the bar, clutching their shopping bags.

"Which way's the station?" Lila was in so much

trouble if she missed her midnight curfew. Her parents would never let her out of the house again.

"About two minutes that way," said Eve, "if we can find a taxi."

The streets all around the bar were absent of any traffic at all. Rushing down the waterfront towards Waterloo, shopping bags bumping against her legs, Lila could only watch the big, shining face of Big Ben over the river, ticking closer and closer to her doom.

"Never mind," said Eve bracingly as Big Ben's chimes boomed through the night air. "We'll cab it to the next stop. Croydon, isn't it?"

"Croydon's miles away," Lila groaned.

Eve patted her bag. "That's why we have credit cards. Follow me."

The taxi driver couldn't believe his luck when Eve requested a ride as far as Croydon. They made it in fifteen minutes, but still missed their connection.

"Another taxi," said Eve, starting to flag one down.

"We can't, it's too expensive." Lila wanted to cry. "There's a bus station over there. See if there's anything going the right way."

They caught a bus that would take them ten

miles from Heartside Bay. Every ten minutes of the journey, Lila gnawed her lip and asked Eve the time. An hour and half later, followed by twenty minutes in the last taxi of the day, and Lila finally found herself outside her own front door. Somewhere in the distance, the town clock chimed two o'clock in the morning.

"I'm sorry," Lila blurted before her parents, waiting silently in the living room, could say a single word. "We missed the train. We—"

"Why can't we trust you to do what we ask?" her father demanded, rising from the sofa. "You take so much from us and give so little back!"

"We tried to call you, Lila," said her mother. "We were worried about you."

"My phone ran out of batteries! I'm sorry, really—"

"Go to bed," said her father wearily. "You need some sleep before your tutor comes in the morning. And we need to discuss what to do with you. Frankly, Lila, I'm running out of ideas."

Lila trailed upstairs to bed. Her feet hurt and her shopping bags were heavy. She couldn't wait to shove them in the back of her wardrobe and collapse on her duvet. Her wonderful, magical day in London already felt like a lifetime ago.

One day, she thought unhappily. *That's all I wanted. Just one day when life actually felt good.*

Reality stunk.

TWELVE

"Tutor's here!"

Sitting bolt upright in bed, Lila rubbed her eyes. Her bedside clock said five to ten. She had a dim memory of her mother waking her up an hour earlier, but she had been so exhausted that she had dropped off again. The tutor was here already?

"Down in five!" she shouted hurriedly.

Catching sight of herself in her bedside mirror, Lila frowned. Her hair was all over the place. As usual, she'd made a poor job of removing her make-up last night. Her eyes were bloodshot and streaked with mascara, while a spot was gathering strength on her chin. She looked a total mess.

Even after her shower – the quickest in history –

Lila felt dull and sluggish. She wiped half-heartedly at her sooty eyes and slapped on a palmful of moisturiser. She pulled on a pair of leggings, a long denim shirt and her favourite slippers. If she had to study for two hours this morning, the least she could be was comfortable. Finally, she brushed her teeth at speed and hurried down the stairs.

"He's in the study," said her mum, handing her a plate of buttered toast.

Lila lifted a piece and crammed it sideways into her mouth.

"Thanks Mum," she mumbled, and pushed open the study door.

She almost choked on her toast as Josh looked up from a sheaf of notes on the table in front of him. He looked gorgeous, in skinny jeans and a leaf-green jumper that brought out the colour of his eyes.

The last time Lila had seen him, she'd been moments from kissing him at the secret beach. She was horribly aware of her scruffy leggings, lemur eyes and wet hair, not to mention the trickle of butter she could feel making its way down her chin.

"Josh?" she said at last. "What are you doing here?"

"Helping you not to flunk your exams next term. I'm your new tutor."

Lila felt a rush of confusing emotions. Part of her was delighted that Josh would be in her house for two hours a day over the entire holidays. The rest of her was wishing him a million miles away.

It could be worse, she thought, wiping the crumbs and butter from around her mouth. *Josh is a friend, not some nerdy stranger. This could even be fun.*

"Sit down," he said, nodding at the sofa.

Lila saluted with a giggle. "Yes sir."

"Just do it, will you? We have a lot to get through this morning."

He looked impatient, tapping his pen on the table. Lila felt a sudden rush of annoyance. He didn't seem in the slightest bit pleased to see her. Why was he being so bossy?

"Sorry for breathing," she said a little sulkily. "You need to lighten up."

"And *you* need to knuckle down. Have you seen your grades lately? A twelve-year-old could produce better work."

Lila felt like she'd been slapped. "Hey," she

objected. "I've only just woken up. Can you just be nice to me for a second?"

Josh folded his arms. "Nice doesn't get results. I'm here to get results."

Lila felt herself squirming before his hard gaze. It was hard to believe that the last time she'd seen him, those same eyes had been as soft as green velvet as he moved to kiss her. Now they looked like emeralds, cold and glittering without any emotion at all.

"Fine," she sighed, sweeping her fringe out of her eyes. "Where do we start?"

"I hear the beginning is good."

He rifled through the scruffy, red-lined papers in front of him, which Lila realized with sudden dismay was the sum total of her work last term. Her eyes pricked with sudden tears.

"Don't be horrible to me, Josh," she begged. "I've had an awful few weeks and I don't deserve this."

"Self-pity won't help," he said brutally. "You are in a total mess, Lila. You need to start digging yourself out."

Lila got to her feet. She found she was trembling. "Why are you being like this?"

Josh looked directly at her. "If you want to ruin your life, go ahead. But you're not going to ruin mine."

Lila groped around for an argument. "But—"

"Don't you get it yet? Mess this year up and what kind of future will you have? I have *plans*. I want to go to university and make something of my life."

Another friend with plans, Lila thought numbly. Didn't anyone know how short life was? How useless it was making plans all the time?

"What about you?" Josh enquired. "What do *you* want to do?"

Lila hated that question so much. "Right now," she spat, "I want you to go away."

"You think I want to be here five days a week during my holidays?" he said, folding his arms. "I worked hard last term. It would be nice to have a break. But this is a job, and I need the money. I am saving for my future. University is expensive. So I'm not going anywhere."

Lila sat down again. She could feel the fight draining out of her.

"What do you want to do with your life, Lila?" Josh repeated, more gently.

Lila rubbed her face. "I don't know," she groaned. "That's half the problem. You're so lucky, Josh. You know what you're good at, and what kind of future you'd like. I don't have a clue."

"You're telling me," he said, with the first flash of humour Lila had seen.

"It's all pointless anyway," she added, slumping back on the sofa. "Ryan's death proved that to me. I just want to live in the moment and forget about the future."

"You don't have that luxury," Josh said. He tapped the papers again. "This proves it. You have to face reality, Lila. Ryan has gone, but you're still here. You can't just switch off."

Lila wished that she *could* switch off. Hit the power button and stop the feelings. She covered her face with her hands.

"I don't want to feel so guilty all the time," she whispered. "Sometimes I think I'll feel like this for ever, and then I'll go mad."

She felt Josh sit beside her. He peeled her hands away from her face.

"Listen to me carefully," he said, looking into her eyes. "Ryan's death was not your fault."

Why did people always say that to her? Didn't they get it?

"Josh, he was showing off because he wanted to impress me!"

Josh held her hands more tightly. "Try and think of it differently. Like, two people messing around at a level crossing. One of them is trying to impress the other by playing chicken on the train rails. Whose fault is the accident that follows?"

His gaze was soft and kind again, behind the glasses that he always wore.

"The guy playing chicken," she said after a moment.

"Right answer."

Lila stared at him. "No one ever put it like that to me before," she said a little wonderingly.

"What can I say? I'm a highly paid tutor. I have valuable brains," he said. "Ryan's death was a horrible accident, Lila. That's all."

He put his arms round her and hugged her. Lila rested her cheek against his shoulder and hugged him back. Something had unknotted deep in her belly.

"Ready to work?" he said, releasing her.

Lila knew this was her last chance. But she wouldn't go down without a fight.

"Only if you promise me something," she said.

He looked a little worried. "What?"

"You help me plan for my future," she said, "and you let me help you chill out more."

Josh sighed. He pushed his glasses up his nose and nodded. "Deal," he said.

"Friends?" Lila said, smiling at him.

"Friends," he agreed.

THIRTEEN

Lila was nodding off over her calculus revision. The sun that was streaming through the study window was warm on her face and hair, and it was so easy to shut her eyes. She'd been up late watching a film on her laptop, with a hero that had looked a bit like Josh. Studying was the last thing she felt like doing this morning.

She felt something flick her ear.

"Ow," she said, startled into opening her eyes.

A rubber band lay on the table in front of her. She stared at it.

"Did you just flick that at me?" she demanded, looking across at Josh.

He sat with his long legs crossed in front of him,

winding another rubber band around his fingers. "You were falling asleep. I woke you up."

"You could have taken my eye out," Lila complained.

"Hardly. Your eyes were closed. Besides," he added, "I'm the Heartside rubber-band-flicking champion. I can hit a fly on a window sill from fifty metres. Your eyes were never in danger."

Lila seized the band and twanged it back. It ricocheted off the frame of Josh's glasses with a nice pinging sound that made her giggle.

"Lila, you have to concentrate," Josh said, sounding a little exasperated. "These facts and figures don't sink into your brain when you lay your head on top of the papers."

"It's too sunny," Lila moaned.

Josh checked his watch. "Half an hour until midday. Finish that paper, and we can hit the town."

Lila perked up at the prospect of getting outside, away from the figures whirling around in her head. "Somewhere we can have fun?"

"Calculus *is* fun," said Josh. He relented at the look on Lila's face. "Fine, we'll go somewhere fun."

Lila wagged her pencil at him. "I choose where."

Josh shook his head. "I choose because I'm your tutor and you have to do what I say."

Lila wished she had another rubber band on hand. "Fine," she said, rolling her eyes. Anything to get away from the tedium of revision.

She forced herself to concentrate on the numbers in front of her. By the time she had reached number ten on the sheet, the answers were forming more quickly than she had expected.

"Got the idea?" Josh said, watching her.

"It's not so bad when you practise lots of them at the same time," she said thoughtfully, totting up another answer.

He raised his hands to the ceiling. "Hallelujah, she's seen the light."

"Not the light, exactly," Lila corrected him. "But maybe the light switch."

When Josh had marked her answers – a pleasing fifteen out of twenty – Lila felt a rush of achievement. Now they had the rest of this gorgeous day to do what they liked. Set against the hard work she'd just put in, the prospect glittered like gold before her.

"We're heading into town, Mum," Lila called into the kitchen, grabbing her sunglasses from the hall table. Josh took his hoodie from the hall stand and shrugged it on.

"Done all your revision?" came the answering call.

"She's done well, Mrs Murray," Josh responded.

Lila smiled gratefully. She needed all the brownie points she could get.

"I wouldn't let her go otherwise," he added.

"Like you could stop me," said Lila, poking him in the side. "You're only my tutor from ten until midday, you know."

They set off for town, their shadows short on the warm pavement. Lila looked furtively at Josh as they walked down the sunny street together. He looked cute in his striped hoodie. Sunglasses had their uses.

"Stop looking at me," said Josh.

"How did you know I was looking at you?" Lila objected, feeling a little put out.

"Because you are as transparent as glass." Looking both ways, he crossed the street at a jog. "Come on or it'll close."

"What'll close?"

"The place I'm taking you to. It closes at one o'clock on Tuesdays."

"Weird time to close," said Lila, puzzled.

"The owner runs an art workshop up at the sixth-form college on Tuesday afternoons," said Josh. "Come on."

Lila started to feel a little nervous. "I don't want to go to an art gallery," she complained, following Josh a little more slowly. "I want to go to the beach. Come on Josh, it's sunny."

"It's not an art gallery," he said, smiling. "You'll love it, I promise. Great, he's still open."

Lila stared across the road at the little bookshop. Its windows were crooked like most of the buildings in this part of the Old Town, the frames painted a fading red. A matching door stood open, propped ajar with a brick.

"A bookshop?" she said.

"Not just any bookshop. The best bookshop in the world."

Lila reluctantly let Josh pull her over the road. His hand felt nice in hers as they ducked through the sloping doorway.

Large shiny books with titles like *Swamp Thing* and *Hellblazer* lined the uneven shelves. The covers were cartoonish and graphic, often boasting more shapes than words.

She folded her arms. "You dragged me out of the sunshine for *comic* books?"

A pained look crossed Josh's face. "Graphic novels," he corrected. "Not comic books. Hey, Mr Spiegelman," he added, raising his hand as a man in a bow tie with a shock of black hair peered around a stack of books at them.

"Josh!" said Mr Spiegelman. "I should have guessed it was you. Who is your friend?"

"This is Lila," Josh said. "She doesn't get graphic novels. I'm trying to open her eyes."

Mr Spiegelman smiled. "Browse away. But remember, Josh—"

"You close in twenty minutes, I know," said Josh. "We won't forget."

Mr Spiegelman disappeared into a back room with a wave of his hand.

"I never said I didn't *get* them," said Lila, feeling like Josh had painted her in a bad light to the guy in the bow tie, who was clearly the owner of the shop. She picked up the nearest book and flicked through the pages to show willing. Pictures and words jumped out at her in a mishmash of speech bubbles and weird perspectives. Something about a raptor, and an amulet, and a chase across a jagged mountain range whose tops were crowned with flashes of lightning.

Silly, Lila thought. She turned the page out of curiosity, to see if the raptor caught the people it was chasing.

"That's one of my favourites."

Lila jumped. Josh had come very close without her realizing.

"See how the artist uses the colour to highlight the mountains?" He pointed. "You get this sense of ominous power. These little guys running through the central panel don't stand a chance, caught between the raptor and the might of the mountains."

"The raptor gets them," Lila guessed.

"Please," said Josh, rolling his eyes. "If it got them, the novel would be over in four pages. What's the point in that? They escape down here. . ."

He showed her the image of a deep crevasse on the

next page. The artist had drawn it at such an angle that the top of the crevasse looked hopelessly inaccessible. Lila wondered what it would feel like to be stuck at the bottom of a hole like that.

". . .where there is a portal here. . ."

She followed Josh's finger as it moved towards a hole in the bottom right-hand corner of the spread.

"That hole glows like the mountains," she said. "Did the artist use the same technique as before?"

"Exactly the same. Fantastic, isn't it? I'll show you another one. It's a bit edgier, but I love it."

He moved among the shelves, homing in on this title and that, showing her brightly coloured action sequences, blue-tinted night scenes, old stuff that looked like the comic strips in her dad's newspapers and new stuff that looked more like album covers than books. The heroes had names like Troy Trouble and Lisa Lowhope; the villains seemed content with just one name plus a title, like Doctor Zen or Professor Abyss. Graphic novels had never been Lila's thing, but it was hard to resist Josh's passion. What would it be like to have a passion like that?

"You're different in here," she said as Josh reached

up to replace a large *Judge Dredd* book he'd been showing her.

"In what way?"

"Evil tutor Josh has been replaced by Having Fun Josh."

Josh made his voice sound supervillain-evil. "Doctor Josh, evil brainiac mastermind, is trying to make the world see how much fun lies in calculus."

Lila giggled, taking up the story. "Little does he know that Lila Lightheart is coming for him in her huge inflatable superhero suit. . ." She puffed out her cheeks and waddled towards him.

"But Doctor Josh has finally perfected the rubber-band gun he has always dreamed of. . ."

". . .leaving Lila Lightheart plummeting to her doom as her suit bursts . . . is this the end for the pumped-up superhero?"

"Time, Josh," called Mr Spiegelman.

"We should draw this," said Josh.

"Yes!" Lila said, enchanted by the idea. "Let's go to the beach and put it together. I'm getting into Lila Lightheart now. I want to know how it ends."

The beach was full of people, drawn out by

the warm sunshine. Boats bobbed on the waves, white sails billowed on the horizon, children made sandcastles and played cricket. Josh sat on the sea wall and pulled out his sketchbook. Lila settled her sunglasses on her nose and sat beside him, her mind sparking with ideas.

"We start with Lila Lightheart having a strange dream in which she eats a bicycle pump," she began. Josh raised his eyebrows, but sketched obediently as Lila made dramatic shapes in the air above her head.

"The bicycle pump has fallen from an alien bicycle," she continued. "It has strange powers. . ."

". . .and tastes curiously like chocolate," Josh added, making Lila snort with laughter.

"In the morning she discovers that she can inflate her clothes and fly around like a hot-air balloon," she continued.

"You are so weird," he said, starting to sketch a figure floating through the sky in a balloon-like superhero suit. "I'm liking this already."

"Make her beautiful," Lila instructed, and leaned over his shoulder to watch the picture take shape.

"Not hard," Josh said.

Lila had a fizzing feeling in her tummy in the silence that followed. *Just friends*, she reminded herself.

"Doctor Josh is turning the whole of Heartside into a black-and-white pit of study misery," she said aloud. "Come on slave, keep up."

Josh laid out three pages peppered with different-sized panels, while Lila made crazy suggestions on how best to fill them. The strange plot twists and turns that they came up with between them made Lila laugh so much that she could hardly breathe. Most of the characters bore a strong resemblance to their friends. There was even a three-winged seagull called Flapjack, Doctor Josh's pet. It flew around in circles quite a lot.

"No more," she groaned, flopping back on the sea wall at last. "My stomach muscles can't take it. Is it finished?"

Josh pressed it into her hands. "All yours," he said. "What are you going to do with it?"

Lila stared at the beautiful, strong pictures spread out so perfectly across the sheets of paper. "I'm going to hang it above my bed," she said impulsively. "To remind me of my superpowers."

"*Our* superpowers," he said. "We can't let Lila Lightheart take all the glory."

Lila felt happier and more at peace than she had for days. She closed her eyes, feeling the warmth of the afternoon sunshine soaking into her skin.

"Josh?"

"Hmm?"

Propping herself up on one elbow, she grinned at him. "It's been a surprisingly good day."

FOURTEEN

"Your turn today," said Josh as Lila closed her English book with a snap and a sigh of relief.

"My turn for what?"

"Your turn to choose what we do this afternoon."

Lila felt ridiculously pleased that Josh wanted to spend another day with her. Then she found herself panicking slightly. What could she come up with that would compare with the fantastic time they'd spent on their comic book the day before?

Her brain whirred through her usual leisure-time options. The cinema was no fun when she wanted to talk – and she always wanted to talk, especially around Josh because he made her laugh. Shopping? Hardly a sport for boys. The Heartbeat?

Why would Josh want to go somewhere he already went most weekends? She had to think of something cool, and original. Nothing was leaping to mind.

Josh linked his hands behind his head as she struggled for ideas. "How about you show me something you're passionate about?" he suggested. "What do you enjoy?"

This was getting worse.

"I enjoy everything, mostly," said Lila. She winced inside. *I sound like the most boring person in the universe*, she thought.

He looked a little puzzled. "Lila, if you don't want to spend another afternoon with me, that's fine. I won't be offended."

"It's not that," Lila said hastily. How could she tell him how much she'd enjoyed yesterday without sounding like a gushing freak? "It's just, I'm not very good at thinking on my feet."

"Tell you what." Josh stood up, brushing biscuit crumbs off his jeans. "Let's get outside and see where we end up. Like a mystery tour."

The feeling of pressure eased a little. "OK," Lila

said gratefully. "Just give me a minute to change, will you?"

In the bathroom, hairbrush in hand, she gave herself a severe talking-to.

"Think," she ordered her reflection. "It's very important Josh doesn't think you're boring."

Why was that so important? she wondered. She didn't know, but it was.

She grabbed some high-waisted jean shorts and pulled on a soft pink tank top. Gold flip-flops and a lick of lip gloss and she was ready. Popping back into her bedroom for a moment to pick up her purse, she took a long look at Josh's comic strip, stuck up in pride of place above her bed. He had so much talent. What talent did she have?

A talent for getting in trouble, she thought.

She could feel a gloomy mood coming on.

"Nice outfit," Josh said as she came down the stairs. "Does it inflate?"

Lila giggled, her mood evaporating. "I wish. There are times when I'd love to fly away from my life. Let's get out of here."

They walked companionably along the road. It was

quieter out today, although a couple of people were walking their dogs. Several kids whizzed past them on scooters and skateboards.

I can't even do that, thought Lila. *I am totally pathetic.*

"You OK?" Josh said, looking at her.

He could read her like one of his graphic novels, she thought.

"Josh," she said before she lost her nerve, "do you think I'm boring?"

He laughed in surprise. "That's hardly a word I'd use to describe you."

"But I don't have any passions," Lila said, blushing. "Nothing I'm crazy about, like you're crazy about drawing and graphic novels. I could tell you a million things I *don't* like, but hardly anything that I *do*."

"Tell me what you don't like, then."

That was easy. "School," Lila began, ticking off the list on her fingers. "My dad when he gets bossy. My dad most days, actually. Dolls. Ponies. Bagpipes."

"I'm really glad you told me. I was thinking of getting us tickets to a Barbie gymkhana in Glasgow."

"I'm serious, Josh," said Lila earnestly. "I don't like *anything*. I'm like a total non-person."

"Of course you're not," said Josh. "You're as real as I am."

Was she? She didn't feel that way, most of the time.

They reached the beach. Lila put her arms round herself, hugging her arms closer to her body and gazed out at the wide, damp expanse of sand.

"Let's build a sandcastle," she said impulsively. "I love doing that."

They bought a castle-shaped bucket and a long-handled spade from one of the beach shops and set about creating an extensive castle with a moat. Lila collected pebbles and shells for decoration, while Josh carved decorative lines into the walls with a stick. The result was pretty magnificent, Lila thought with satisfaction.

"Maybe I could go into sandcastle architecture," she said as they sat beside their castle and watched the tide curling towards them.

"I hear there's a big demand for that in the Sahara Desert," said Josh. "You shouldn't be so hard on yourself, Lila. Sometimes it takes time for people to find what they're good at."

Lila drew in the sand with her finger. "I'm good at winding my parents up. It's a shame I can't make a career of that." Her dad hadn't gotten home last night until late and she had already been in bed, but she wasn't looking forward to the discussion she knew they were going to have to have eventually about her broken curfew.

"Have you always been a rebel?" Josh asked.

Lila shrugged. "It goes with the territory. I'm a police chief's daughter."

"You've been so busy rebelling against the world that you've forgotten to look inside yourself for your own talents," he said.

Lila stared at him. He had it exactly right. "How do you know these things?" she demanded.

Josh didn't answer. He lay back in the sand. "Tell me more about the things you don't like."

It was easy, opening up to Josh. Lila wondered why she'd never done it before.

"I don't want some boring life in Heartside," she said with certainty. "I don't want to be known as Chief Murray's troublemaking daughter either."

Josh squinted up at her through the sunlight. "Do you want to get married? Have children?"

Lila couldn't imagine having kids. "No way," she said, shaking her head. "How can I be a mum without knowing who I am? Anyway, all you're doing by having kids is replacing the population. The planet's too full already. Don't you think?"

"Maybe, but if I agree, I'm effectively saying that I shouldn't have been born and nor should you. So I'll stay quiet."

Lila lay down beside him. They stayed like that for a while, side by side on the sand, listening to the waves and the gulls and the occasional barking dog.

"I feel like I'm destined for something more than this place can give me," Lila said, gazing up at the clouds overhead. "But I don't have the faintest idea what."

"Good. So you can start making plans."

Propping herself up on one elbow, Lila looked at Josh in confusion. What was he talking about now? "How can I plan for nothing?" she demanded.

"Work hard. Do the best you can, at everything you

can. Then, when you do figure out what you want to do, you're all set."

"I don't understand," said Lila.

He propped himself up as well. His green eyes were clear and serious through his glasses. "Let's say you flunk biology, and then realize you want to be a life scientist. Bang, your chance is gone. Or you suddenly realize engineering is your favourite thing, only you blew your maths GCSE."

"OK," Lila said, trying to follow Josh's argument.

"You have to be patient," he said. "Keep your options open. And you have to study harder and do better in school, so those options stay open, for as long as it takes. You'll work out what you want in the end."

"But that's so boring," Lila moaned.

"Do you want to make something of your life, or not?"

Lila sighed. Josh was right, as usual. "Fine," she said. "I'll work harder."

In a funny way, she felt relieved. As if she'd given herself permission to make an effort, to not give up on herself.

If Josh is going to make it out of Heartside and make a great life for himself, she thought with sudden resolve, *I will too.*

FIFTEEN

Lila buckled down on Wednesday night and did half an hour's preparation for her tutoring session on history with Josh in the morning. She'd always enjoyed history, but the past few weeks were a blur of nothing. She did her best to pick up the story where she'd left off paying attention. Soon she was engrossed in the spidery details of the Cold War, with all its secrets and its spying and its near-disastrous nuclear experiments.

"Have you been revising?" Josh asked in surprise the following morning. "That's three correct facts you've given me, and it's not even ten-thirty yet."

"I have no idea what you mean," Lila said primly. "I'm just naturally gifted at these things."

Pacing up and down the study, Josh started firing questions at her.

"When did they build the Berlin Wall?"

"1961."

"When did they take it down again?"

"1989."

"What was the name of the Stanley Kubrick film about the Cold War, made in 1964?"

"*Dr Strangelove*."

"Have you ever seen it?"

Lila blinked. "No. Should I have?"

"It's a good film. I have a copy of it. We should watch it sometime."

Lila's stomach flipped. "OK," she said.

It wouldn't be a date, she reminded herself as Josh handed her some study questions. *Just two friends watching a film.*

Noon came surprisingly fast. As Lila packed up her books, she wondered if Josh would suggest spending the day together again. As he went to fetch his jacket from the hall stand, her phone rang.

"Good timing, Rhi," Lila said, cradling her phone between her ear and her shoulder. "I've just finished this morning's tutoring session with Josh."

"And . . . how are you two getting on?"

Lila detected a teasing hint in Rhi's tone of voice.

"The tutoring's going really well," she said. "Thanks for asking."

"I don't mean the tutoring. How are *you two* getting on?"

"Rhi, Josh and I just are friends. He's tutoring me so I don't mess up my future. That's all there is to it."

Rhi sounded unconvinced. "If you say so. Listen, are you two busy this afternoon?"

Lila felt excited. "Why, what's up?"

"Brody and I are recording a new demo at mine. Brody's borrowed all this recording equipment, so it's going to be great! Do you and Josh want to come along?"

"What's the plan?" said Josh, pulling on his jacket as Lila hung up.

"Rhi and Brody are recording a demo at Rhi's house. Sounds like Rhi wants an audience."

Josh nodded. "I'm in if you are."

Lila felt a flush of warmth running over her skin. "Sure you're not bored with me yet?" she said teasingly, hoping not to see his eyes flicker.

"Not yet," he said, smiling at her.

Lila felt herself relaxing.

Rhi's house was a little way up the hill, towards the golden cliffs that overlooked Heartside Bay. Lila felt a little breathless as they reached the blue front door. Josh walked quickly. She had no particular memory of the walk – just that it had flown by. Time always did, with Josh.

"Hey!" Rhi smiled at them as she opened the front door. Her hair stood out around her head in a pretty cloud and she was wearing long dangly earrings that almost reached her shoulders. She had her usual touch of make-up on, and a top Lila had never seen her wear before. It looked like she was making an effort for Brody. Lila smiled to herself.

Brody was perched on the end of Rhi's bed, lightly strumming his guitar. A mice stood by the window, along with a neat little recording deck attached to a computer. He greeted them with his usual wide smile.

"Hope you don't mind us being here, Brody," said Lila, suddenly feeling shy. She'd heard him sing at the

Heartbeat more often than she'd spoken to him, and found that she was a little star-struck this close. "Rhi asked us."

"Music always sounds better with an audience," he said.

"You have to be really quiet," Rhi said, ushering them into two chairs that she had arranged by the door. The room wasn't very big. "Promise?"

Lila watched Rhi and Brody consult over the music and then tune their guitars so that they were pitched perfectly. *More friends with a clear idea of their future*, she thought. She felt the familiar swell of jealousy deep in her belly.

Josh glanced at her. "You'll get there soon," he said. "Be patient."

He was doing it again. Reading her like she was going around with subtitles over her head. Lila felt unsettled at the thought of being so transparent.

"OK," said Rhi, "so the first one we're going to lay down is 'Sweet Summer'. We sang it at the Heartbeat's opening night."

Lila remembered how Ollie and Polly had been dancing together to the romantic lilt of the rhythm that night, and how sad it had made her feel. She nodded. "Sure. It's a great song."

Brody hit a button on the computer, and counted them in with silent fingers.

"Sweet summer," he began, "lazy haze, dancing beside you without counting the days. . ."

Rhi joined in, the harmonies so smooth it was as if she'd been singing all along.

"Grass on our skin, sun in the sky, sweet summer, asking us why, sweet summer, making us cry, sweetest of all of the summers. . ."

"Never was summer so sweet," Brody sang back.

Lila watched, entranced by the magic unfolding in front of her. She could smell the grass, feel the heat . . . sense the love. Something told her it wasn't just the words making her feel that way. It was the clear attraction between Rhi and Brody as they sang.

"Sweet summer, darkening sky now," Brody sang.

"Moon on the wane, saying goodbye now," Rhi sang back.

"Sweet summer, asking us why, sweet summer, making us cry. . ."

"Sweetest of all of the summers," they sang, their

heads so close they were touching, "never was summer so sweet. Never, never was summer so sweet."

Lila sensed Josh holding his breath beside her as the delicate plucking of the guitar strings faded away. Brody and Rhi were looking at each other in a way that made Lila feel like she and Josh shouldn't be there.

Two heavy seconds of silence followed the end of the song.

Rhi suddenly leaned towards Brody and kissed him on the cheek. "Best we've ever done it," she said.

Lila wasn't sure who made the first move. But somehow Brody's and Rhi's lips had met.

The bedroom door flew back on its hinges, making everyone jump. To Lila's horror, Max was standing there. For once, he wasn't smiling. In fact, his whole face was suffused with shock as he stared at Rhi and Brody.

"This is awkward," Josh murmured in Lila's ear. She would have enjoyed the warmth of his breath against her skin if it hadn't been for the circumstances.

Rhi pulled back from Brody's. Her cheeks were fiery. "Max?" she stammered. "What . . . what are you doing here?"

"I might ask you the same question." The glare Max threw at Brody was red hot.

"We're recording," said Brody. He picked up his guitar again. "Among other things."

This was beyond embarrassing. Lila wished she and Josh were somewhere else.

From the look on her friend's stricken face, Rhi was wishing much the same. "But what are you doing here, Max?" she repeated helplessly.

"Showing your dad the new website promoting the Heartbeat." Max was still glaring daggers at Brody. "But of course, that's a lot less interesting than what's going on in here."

"I didn't mean for that to happen, we just got caught up in the moment. . . Max, please don't get upset—"

"Upset?" Max repeated incredulously. He jabbed in Brody's direction. "You're snogging Surfer Boy over there, and I'm not supposed to get upset? How long have you been kissing my girlfriend?" he asked Brody.

"Chill out, man," said Brody. He lightly strummed the strings. "It was only a kiss. Rhi and I just got a little carried away in the moment."

Max made a snarling noise deep in his throat, lifted his fist and threw a punch right into Brody's face.

"Stop!" Lila gasped, jumping to her feet as Brody and Max tumbled to the ground, arms locked around each other, Max's fists flailing in the air. "Josh, stop them!"

Josh was already halfway across the room, his arms extended to yank Max to his feet. Rhi grasped Brody by the arm and pulled him upright.

Brody rubbed his jaw, which was already showing the promise of a bruise. "You need to lighten up, man," he said, still sounding remarkably calm. "I don't want any hassle, OK? I just want to make music."

"That wasn't music you were making," Max spat, struggling in Josh's arms.

"Max, please!" Rhi begged, close to tears. "Please don't make this worse than it already is. Brody. . ." she swung round to look at him, "I'm sorry I kissed you, I don't know what came over me."

Brody was still rubbing his jaw. "You have to decide, Rhi. Are you serious about this music partnership or not? If you are, you have to focus. This is my life. I thought you wanted it to be your life too."

Lila watched Rhi wrestling with her decision.

"Max," she said tentatively, "I'm sorry, I really am. But . . . you and I are over. We've been over for a while. I'm sorry I kissed you last week, that was a mistake. I'm really serious about making it work with Brody. I can't have distractions like this." She rubbed her hands miserably through her hair. "Can't we just be friends?"

At last, Lila thought. But she couldn't muster much enthusiasm. She'd never seen Max look so stricken.

"It's not that I want to go out with Brody," Rhi went on beseechingly, "but I do want to play with him, and record songs with him, and have some kind of professional future with him."

"You're choosing *him*?" said Max in astonishment.

Lila wondered if he'd ever been dumped by a girl before.

"I'm not choosing him," Rhi said. "I'm choosing myself."

Max still looked unhappy. Brody's face was as calm as ever.

"Good for you, Rhi," said Josh unexpectedly. "Now, why don't we all shake hands and make friends?"

Brody extended his hand amiably in Max's direction. "This isn't about us, man. It's about the music."

Max ignored the hand, turned on his heel and left the bedroom. Rhi giggled. Lila guessed it was the nerves.

"Sorry about that, everyone," she said. "Did the song sound OK?"

"It sounded gorgeous and you know it," said Lila.

Rhi looked wistfully at the door. "I really want to stay friends with Max," she said.

"I don't think he's ready for that yet," Lila told her.

She glanced at Josh. Thank goodness *they* had got over that weird little glitch at the beach and were still friends. She couldn't take any more drama in her life.

SIXTEEN

Lila, Rhi and Polly stood outside Eve's front door, shivering in the evening wind.

"Max must really hate me now," Rhi moaned, for about the hundredth time since the girls had met up at the Heartbeat half an hour earlier.

Lila was in the mood for fun, not misery and regret. "Rhi," she said impatiently, "try to remember that you ended it with Max weeks ago. If Max wants to overreact by hitting Brody, that's his problem. Remember what Josh said when you made that speech about choosing yourself instead of Max? He said 'Good for you'. And I agree with him."

"I can't believe Max actually punched Brody," said Polly, wide-eyed.

Lila remembered the sound of Max's fist hitting Brody's jaw. "Josh was amazing, the way he broke up the fight," she said. "Why do boys have to complicate things? Rhi was only having a kiss. Weren't you?"

Rhi blushed. "I still don't know how it happened," she said.

"I do." Lila gave a dramatic swoon, her hand to her forehead. "You and Brody looked into each other's eyes and couldn't resist each other. . ."

Rhi blushed. "You're full of rubbish, Lila."

"Was he a good kisser?" Polly asked, giggling.

Rhi's face grew a little redder. "Um, yes. Yes, he was."

Lila stamped her feet. It really was cold out here. Her good mood threatened to freeze along with her toes. Where was Eve? They'd rung the doorbell twice already but no one was answering. She checked her watch. Ten past eight.

"Eve did say eight, didn't she?" she checked with the others.

Polly nodded. "Apparently Eve's cooking something."

Lila made a face. "Seriously?"

She couldn't imagine Eve doing anything in the

kitchen beyond putting bread into the toaster, most likely with silver toast tongs. She gazed up at the pillars that framed the front of Eve's house. They reminded her of Eve's father's club.

The door opened. Eve, looking a little pink in the face, waved them inside with a wooden spoon. "Sorry! I keep forgetting Yelitza's on holiday – she normally opens the door."

Lila had been to Eve's house several times before, but each time, it looked a little different. Eve's mother liked redecorating on a regular basis. Today, the wide entrance hall was painted a delicate duck-egg blue with a new glass chandelier hanging from the ceiling.

"Nice chandelier," said Polly, looking upwards. "Vintage?"

"I don't know," Eve said vaguely. "Mummy got it in Paris. Come into the kitchen."

Something smelled delicious, Lila noticed. Perhaps Eve could cook after all. A younger version of Eve looked up from scanning through what looked like a fashion magazine on a tablet at the kitchen table.

"Hello," said Chloe, Eve's sister. Her eyes were a darker grey than Eve's, her long auburn hair pulled back in a plait. She scanned Lila's outfit. "I like your dress," she concluded, "but I don't think the shoes work with it."

Lila looked down uncertainly at her green dress. She had liked how she'd combined it with her black Converse. She thought it looked good.

"Ignore Chloe," Eve said. "She's very precocious. Go away, infant, if you can't be nice to my friends."

"It's not a crime to take an interest in fashion," said Chloe. "And I'm not an infant. I'm only eighteen months younger than you."

Lila wasn't sure she liked Chloe much. *You didn't like Eve much either at first*, she reminded herself. She knew she ought to give Chloe a chance.

Eve put her wooden spoon down and wiped her hands on the spotless white apron that she wore. "I just have to check something in the oven and then we can go through to the snug," she said. "I've got snacks."

"It smells really good, Eve," said Rhi, sniffing appreciatively as the oven door opened in a gust of sweetly scented steam. "What is it?"

Eve picked up a cardboard lid from the grey granite

work surface. "Moroccan tagine with lemon and cumin," she read off the packaging.

"I thought you said you were cooking tonight!" Polly accused.

Eve looked puzzled. "I *am* cooking," she said, waving the packaging under Polly's nose.

Lila exchanged amused looks with Rhi and Polly. For Eve, putting an expensive ready meal in the oven probably did qualify as cooking.

"Mummy can't cook either," said Chloe.

Lila hoped Mrs Somerstown wasn't around tonight. She'd always found Eve's mother as chilly as a block of ice.

"Don't worry, she's not back from her gym class yet," said Chloe, accurately reading Lila's expression.

"Thank goodness," said Eve. "Ever since the whole business about You Know What, Mummy acts like I'm a strange wild animal loose in her house."

"You *can* say lesbian, Eve," scoffed Chloe.

Lila and the others looked at each other. Eve hadn't said much about how her sister had taken the news that she was gay.

"Chloe's been very supportive," Eve put in, seeing

their worried looks. "Daddy's been brilliant of course. It's just Mummy who's still struggling with it."

The front door slammed.

"That is the *last* time I go to that spin class," came a voice from the hall. "The changing rooms are simply disgusting and my head is splitting. Where's Yelitza?"

"Yelitza's on holiday, Mummy," Eve said as Mrs Somerstown wafted into the kitchen in an expensive-looking pale grey tracksuit. "Remember?"

Mrs Somerstown looked irritated. "It's very inconvenient of her to leave us like this," she said. She didn't even look at Lila, Rhi or Polly. "I intend to talk to your father about it."

Lila noticed how Eve brightened at the mention of her father. "Is Daddy coming home later?" she asked eagerly.

Mrs Somerstown looked more irritated than ever. "For heaven's sake, don't ask me. You father never tells me anything. I'm going to have a bath. I swear, I'm going to catch something nasty from that gym one of these days. You'd think, for the price of membership, they would employ staff who knew how to polish taps. Mind you and your friends don't make too much noise."

She wafted out again.

There was a strained silence.

"Don't mind Mummy," said Eve at last. She ushered Lila, Rhi and Polly into the snug. "She's had a difficult week."

Lila couldn't help wondering what it must be like, living with a mother like Mrs Somerstown. She shivered a little at the thought.

In the snug, Eve had laid out several pretty dishes with snacks and crackers, and a jug of cold lemonade.

"I'm sorry it's not home-made," she said a little fretfully, pouring everyone a glass. "We're a bit lost without Yelitza."

"When's she coming back?" asked Polly.

Eve sank on to one of the big white sofas. She looked weary. "Between you and me, I don't think she's coming back at all."

If I worked for Mrs Somerstown, I'd leave too, Lila thought.

"Why not?" asked Rhi.

Eve fiddled with the glass of lemonade in her hand.

"Yelitza's taken a lot more of her stuff than you would normally take for a holiday. I checked."

"You checked?" said Polly, mystified. "Why?"

"I think Daddy's having money troubles," Eve confessed. "He's already sold the yacht, and a few of his vintage cars. Staff are expensive, so it would make sense to stop employing Yelitza. You've probably noticed how we're slumming it a bit at the moment."

Lila looked around at the plush snug. It didn't look very slummy to her, but she wasn't used to the things Eve was used to.

"Josh would say, make the best of what you have," she said aloud.

"You keep bringing up Josh tonight," said Rhi, looking curiously at Lila. "Ever since we met at the Heartbeat earlier it's been Josh said this, Josh thinks that. What's going on with you two?"

"Nothing!" Flushing a little, Lila took a long drink of her lemonade. "We're friends. It is possible for a girl and a boy to be friends, you know."

Polly, Eve and Rhi exchanged loaded glances.

• "Don't pull faces like that!" Lila protested. "It's true."

"Why are you fighting this?" Polly asked. "It's so obvious you two should get together."

"You have been spending a lot of time with him lately," Rhi added. "And he definitely likes you."

"And he is very cute," Eve added. "You know, for a boy."

"He's my tutor! It wasn't my idea for him to come round to my house every day of the holidays. You're making too much of this." Lila felt hot and flustered, and a little irritated at the knowing smiles on the others' faces. "We're just friends, OK? Can we drop it now?"

SEVENTEEN

Josh was cute, Lila supposed, looking at him now as he went over once again the theory of calculus in the light pouring through the study window on Friday morning. If you liked tall skinny nerds who wore nice colours and had kind eyes. Which she didn't.

"And of course," Josh concluded, "calculus was fundamental in explaining how aliens came to found Heartside High in the nineteen fifties."

"Uh huh," said Lila, absently jotting it down.

Josh snorted with laughter. "I knew you weren't listening."

Lila looked at the paper on the table in front of her. *Aliens*, she'd written. *Heartside High*. She flushed with embarrassment and scribbled them out. "Sorry," she said, hoping he wouldn't ask what she'd been thinking about. "What gave me away?"

"Your eyes. They change colour when you daydream."

Lila was surprised. Both by this fact about her eyes, and that Josh had noticed.

"What colour to they go?" she asked curiously.

"A darker blue," he said. "Like the deepest part of the sea."

"You old romantic," Lila grinned, deciding to embarrass him the way he'd embarrassed her with the alien thing. She propped her chin in her hands and fluttered her lashes at him. "Tell me something else about my eyes."

Josh sat down beside her and studied her with a look of deep concentration. His eyes were even greener, this close up. Lila felt a little light-headed. If she reached out, she could cup his face in her hands and—

"There are two of them," Josh concluded, sitting back.

Sometimes Lila could have quite happily murdered Josh. "That's not what I meant," she said with a pout.

"You shouldn't fish for compliments," he said, standing up again. "You know perfectly well your eyes are killer pretty."

Killer pretty. It was suddenly as if Lila was back on the secret beach again, Josh's arms around her and his mouth moments away from hers. She stared at him and he stared back. The study felt strangely small.

"Calculus," said Josh suddenly. "We should be talking about calculus."

Lila didn't want to talk about calculus. "Your eyes are like the green pebbles I sometimes find on the beach," she said. "Only shinier."

Josh rubbed his head with his hands. "Can we change the subject? And get back to what I'm being paid for?"

Lila pulled herself together. "Of course," she said, picking up her pencil again. "As you were, Mr Tutor."

"Calculus," Josh began again. He sat down at the table and adjusted his glasses. "Actually, forget calculus. Let's talk about something else. Algebra."

"Algebra," Lila repeated obediently.

Killer pretty. The words bounced around in her head like little rubber balls.

Josh put a sheet of paper on the table in front of her. "Twenty quadratic equations by midday," he said.

Lila took the paper. Her fingers touched his. Lila felt such an intense reaction that she half expected the desk lamp to flicker and fuse.

This has to stop or everything will be ruined, she thought.

"Josh," she blurted, "are you sure you're OK about the friends thing?"

"Yes," he replied firmly. "Friends is good. I'm very happy with friends. Are you happy with friends?"

Was she?

"Of course I'm happy with friends," she said aloud. "Friends is so much easier than anything else, isn't it?"

He nodded. "Definitely."

"Have you ever had a girlfriend, Josh?" Lila asked curiously.

He looked embarrassed. "Depends on how you define girlfriend."

No, in other words, Lila thought. He really was

very cute. He'd make a perfect boyfriend for someone who wasn't her.

"What about you?" Josh asked. "Boyfriends, I mean?"

"Two proper ones," Lila said. "Lots of flings. Nothing much in between. I never seem to find the right guy." She was struck by a sudden brilliant idea. "Why don't we organize a double date?"

"What?"

"I find someone I think you'll like," Lila explained, "and you find someone for me. Then we all go out together and have fun. Oh my gosh, I have the *perfect* girl for you in my mind already."

"No pressure then," said Josh. "Fine. Let's do it on Saturday. I should be able to find someone for you by then. Now will you please concentrate on those algebra questions?"

They were only on their first course, and Lila was already wishing she'd chosen a different restaurant. Candles and cute checked tablecloths were fine, but only if you fancied the guy sitting opposite you. If you didn't, they were a little overwhelming. Her pasta wasn't even very nice.

"Do you like chess, Lily?" asked Tyler, his fork halfway to his mouth.

He'd been calling her Lily all evening. She couldn't be bothered to correct him.

"Sing me one of their songs, and I'll tell you," she quipped, trying her best to lighten the tone.

Tyler's thick eyebrows beetled together in confusion. "Chess isn't a band."

Help, Lila thought. She glanced sideways to see how Josh was getting on with Sasha.

"So you draw?" Sasha was saying. "Can you do horse legs? They're the hardest things, aren't they?"

"I do more alien life forms than horses, if I'm honest," Josh replied.

Lila shot him a sympathetic look. *Sorry for putting you through this*. This wasn't working out the way she'd hoped at all.

"Lily thinks chess is a band," said Tyler, looking at Josh for assistance.

"They *are* a band," said Josh without missing a beat. "Early seventies, psychedelic rock. Surely you've heard of them?"

Lila giggled. Good old Josh, to the rescue as always.

"I was playing chess down in Southampton last weekend," said Sasha unexpectedly.

Tyler looked properly at Sasha. "You were?"

With her long blonde curls and pink-painted fingernails, Sasha didn't look much like a typical chess player. Lila had never heard her mention it in the gym class they shared. She forked up some pasta and tucked it carefully into her mouth between bright red lips. "It was only a regional," she said. "Do you play, Tyler?"

"A little," said Tyler. His pale skin had turned pink. "Well, maybe more than a little. Do you play in a team?"

The conversation was suddenly peppered with chess phrases that Lila had trouble understanding: bishop pair, active defence, simultaneous play. Josh looked just as baffled.

"I do debating too," Sasha continued when they'd run out of chess anecdotes.

Tyler looked more excited than ever. "I've always wanted to do debating."

"That makes one of us," said Lila, doing her best to stay in the conversation. "I never have anything interesting to say."

Josh snorted into his soda. Tyler looked confused all over again. Sasha gave a polite smile and went back to her pasta.

"I'm going to the bathroom," Lila said. "Don't have too much fun without me."

She wondered how long she could stay in the bathroom without it looking suspicious. Why had she arranged tonight? Sasha didn't fit Josh *at all*. And Tyler . . . what had Josh been thinking?

She almost bumped into Josh outside the bathroom.

"Enjoying yourself?" he asked.

"Not exactly," she sighed, tucking her long dark hair behind her ears. "It's like wading through treacle out there, isn't it?"

"For us, maybe," Josh agreed. "Sasha and Tyler seem to be having a good time though."

"At least someone is," Lila said gloomily.

When they got back to the table, Tyler and Sasha were both pulling their coats on.

"Thanks for arranging this evening," Sasha said,

looking at Lila. "But I have to go. I've missed the last bus and Tyler said he'd walk me home. Do you mind?"

Lila felt a wash of relief. "Of course not. That's really kind of you, Tyler."

Tyler blushed. "I live near Sasha so it's no trouble. I've left some money on the table for the food."

"Goodbye, Josh," said Sasha, holding out her hand politely. Josh shook it.

"See you in geometry class, Josh," said Tyler. "Nice to meet you, Lily."

"He doesn't live anywhere near Sasha," said Josh in amusement as Sasha and Tyler left the restaurant together. "She was telling me she lives up by the cliff. He's in the Old Town, not far from me."

What a classic ending to a terrible date. Lila could feel the onset of giggles.

"Come on, Lily," said Josh, giving her a gentle shove between the shoulder blades. "Let's go and hide our blushes on the beach."

Lila had always loved the beach at night. The seagulls were asleep, so for once all they could hear were the gentle shushing waves.

"Promise me you'll never arrange anything like that again," said Josh as they walked together to the edge of the water.

Lila groaned. "I'm so sorry. I thought you'd like Sasha because she's brainy."

"And I thought you'd like Tyler because his eyebrows look like caterpillars."

Lila exploded into giggles, grabbing Josh's hand playfully. "They totally did! I wonder what kind of butterflies they would turn into?"

"Very large ones," said Josh. "You know, I think we should be proud of ourselves tonight. We picked the perfect dates. Just not for each other."

He was still holding her hand, loose and comfortable. Lila let him. It felt safe, and natural.

What's going on? she wondered a little uneasily. She couldn't possibly be attracted to Josh. He was brainy and super-sensible. OK, he could be funny, but he was basically a school nerd. The exact opposite of her type.

He suddenly stopped and looked down at her in the moonlight. Lila's heart almost jumped out of her mouth. What would she do if he kissed her now?

"I'm so glad we're friends," he said.

Lila felt strangely irritated. She forced a smile on to her face.

"Me too," she replied.

EIGHTEEN

Lila felt strangely restless on Sunday. She couldn't settle down to anything.

"You're like a lost soul today," her mother remarked as she poked listlessly at the toaster late on Sunday afternoon. "Is everything all right?"

"Everything's fine, Mum," she said, irritated by the worried tone in her mother's voice.

"How did last night's date with Josh go?"

It was always deeply embarrassing when her parents took too close an interest in her love life. "It wasn't a date with Josh," she said through gritted teeth. "It was a date with a friend of Josh. And it went so well that he left with another girl."

"Too bad," said her mother.

"Too bad?" Lila echoed. "The guy was a nerd, Mum."

"Why did you go out with him if you didn't like him?"

Lila was in no mood for an interrogation. Deciding to ignore her mother's question, she took her toast upstairs to eat in the privacy of her bedroom.

Tyler and Sasha are probably out on a date already, she thought, munching on her toast and gazing out of her bedroom window at the street below. Why did it work out for everyone else, but never her?

There was nothing on TV. She couldn't find the energy to upload a film. She flicked through a couple of magazines, then tried a few rounds of Angry Birds. Just as she thought she was going to die of boredom, her phone vibrated.

Need you at the Heartbeat NOW!
P x

Lila felt a stirring of interest. Hitting the dial button, she called Polly. All she got was an engaged tone. What was going on?

Her phone vibrated again.

Really important. Come ASAP!

P x

Lila called Polly's number for a second time. Still engaged. Since when did Polly text and call at the same time? What was happening at the Heartbeat?

She tried Eve and Rhi's phones. No answer.

"Fine," said Lila aloud. "I'm coming."

She went through her wardrobe to choose something cleaner than the ratty old jeans she'd been wearing. Her eyes settled on her silver ballet pumps, a lacy white top she'd bought a couple of weeks ago, and some bright pink skinny jeans.

I need a little colour in my life, she thought, fixing her favourite earrings and tousling her hair around her head. She was feeling better already, she realized. She applied her mascara and a swipe of lip gloss, grabbed her bag and headed downstairs.

"Going out?" said her father, putting his head round the door.

Wasn't it obvious? "Yes, Dad. Don't worry, I won't be late," she said impatiently. "And before you ask, I've done my preparation for Josh's tutoring tomorrow, OK?"

She hurried into the darkening evening, pulling her jacket a little more tightly around herself. What could be happening at the Heartside? A surprise gig with Rhi and Brody? She ran through her friends' birthdays in her head. None of them were even close.

The Heartbeat looked quiet and dark. Lila paused in the doorway, looking uncertainly through the glass. Now she came to think of it, the Heartbeat was usually closed on a Sunday night.

The door opened suddenly, making Lila jump.

"Hi!" said Rhi brightly. She was wearing an apron, her hair scraped away from her face in a brightly coloured scarf. "Come in, quickly." She propelled Lila through the empty main room towards the steps that led to the roof garden. "Up there, go on."

Lila sniffed the air. She could smell fat herby sausages grilling somewhere. Her tummy rumbled. The toast already felt a long time ago.

"Is it a party?" she asked.

"Kind of," said Rhi. "Round the corner, there you go . . . nearly there."

The last time Lila had been on these steps, she'd been hand in hand with Robbie/Nick who'd turned out to be Luke. She had a sudden, uneasy feeling in her belly as Rhi pushed her through the door to the roof garden.

At first, all Lila could see was a forest of flickering candles. They were everywhere: on the wall surrounding the garden, lining the paths, hanging in lanterns from the trellises. It lent the little garden an air of a place out of time. The smell of sausages was stronger up here. Lila noticed a little glowing barbecue beside a small wooden table set for two with a basket of bread, a bowl of salad, some olives and a large bottle of sparkling water.

Polly and Eve loomed out of the darkness. Polly was wearing an apron like Rhi. Eve was in black and white with a little bow tie like a restaurant manager, her auburn hair secured neatly at the nape of her neck.

Lila sank into the chair Eve had pulled out for her. "What are we celebrating?" she said, gazing around the roof garden in bewilderment.

"*We're* not celebrating anything," said Rhi. She produced a little bell which she stood on the table beside the basket of bread. "If you need anything, madam, don't hesitate to ring this and we'll attend to your needs."

"Right now I need an explanation!" Lila said. Eve, Rhi and Polly were all being maddeningly mysterious.

Polly's eyes twinkled in the candlelight. "Just promise to go with it, OK?"

"Go with what? Guys? *Guys!*"

The roof door shut, leaving Lila all alone with the sizzle of the sausages. She sat completely still, trying to process what was happening.

The roof door opened again.

"It's about time you came back," said Lila, turning round. "Can someone please explain—"

The words died in her throat.

"Lila?" Josh looked mystified as he looked around the candlelit roof garden. "What's going on?"

"You mean, you don't know either?" asked Lila, recovering from the shock of seeing him.

"I just got a call half an hour ago telling me to dress up and come to the Heartbeat." He brushed something off the dark jacket he was wearing. "The door was open downstairs, so I came in. Rhi and Polly and Eve practically pushed me up the steps. What are you doing here?"

The jigsaw fell into place.

"They've set us up," Lila said in amazement.

"They what?"

Lila sat down at the table again, suddenly. "They've set us up on a date, Josh." She stared at the sausages on the glowing barbecue, the cold beaded bottle on the table.

"Wow," said Josh. He scratched his head. "They have?"

Lila suddenly saw a piece of paper on the table, tucked underneath the bottle of water.

Hi you two. You were never going to do it, so we've done it for you. Don't be mad. Enjoy yourselves. You're meant to be together.

xx

"We'd better not disappoint them then," said Josh, startling Lila out of her thoughts as he read the paper over her shoulder. "Had we?"

Lila suddenly felt very glad that she'd changed out

of her old jeans. She grinned at him. "Sausage?" she said.

The sausages were delicious, a little burned and crispy on the outside but juicy inside. Together with the bread and salad, they made a perfect meal.

"This is a lot nicer than the pasta last night," Lila said as they ate.

"The company's better too," Josh replied.

Lila could hardly believe it. Josh was flirting with her. It felt weird but wonderful.

Soon most of the food was all gone, leaving only a few fronds of lettuce in the salad bowl. As they talked over the last pieces of bread, Lila heard music coming from a speaker balanced precariously on a bench near their table.

"Great song," she said. "Who's it by?"

"I think it's by Chess," said Josh seriously.

Lila exploded with laughter. "Oh my gosh, do you remember Tyler's face when I said that?"

"I don't want to talk about Tyler. I want to dance with you. Are you prepared to take the risk?" Lila's heart thudded as Josh reached over the table and took her hand.

"I am if you are," she joked, trying to ignore the flutter in her stomach.

It was lovely to feel Josh's arms around her. She snuggled in deeper as the music played. Why had she never danced with him before? They seemed to . . . fit.

"Josh," she said, pulling back to look up at him. "*Did* you write me those lovely anonymous letters, in my first week in Heartside? I feel like you did, but you've never said so."

"I have no idea what you're talking about," he replied, smiling slightly.

He bent his head and kissed her. Contrary to Lila's expectations, he wasn't hesitant at all.

NINETEEN

"Nineteen times fourteen."

Lila wound her arms a little more tightly around Josh's neck. "Six hundred and eighty six."

Josh pushed her arms down. "Concentrate. You're miles off. Nineteen times fourteen."

"*Five* hundred and eighty-six," Lila said, running her hands up the hairs on the back of Josh's neck. They felt lovely and soft.

"Now you're just winding me up. *Estimate* it, Lila. Twenty times fourteen, take away the extra fourteen, it's easy."

"It's not easy when you're holding me," Lila said, grinning.

Josh sighed and pushed her hands down again. "I'm

162

not holding *you*. You're holding *me*. I'll give you a clue two hundred and. . ."

"Eighty-six."

She wished he would kiss her again instead of ask her maths questions. Last night they had kissed for what felt like hours. Josh had told her how beautiful she was, and how he'd liked her for such a long time, and how he couldn't believe he was kissing her at last. Things a girl liked to hear. She wanted to hear more. But he was being annoyingly professional today, only giving her a brief peck on the cheek when she had flung open the door for their morning's tutoring session almost two hours earlier. Now it was all business, business, business. No fun at all.

She made a grab for his hands as he reached for a set of maths questions. "Kiss me," she demanded.

"You are impossible," he said, half smiling. "We haven't got through half what we needed to do today, and our time runs out in twenty minutes."

"Kiss me or I won't answer any more questions."

He stared at her in exasperation. Stubbornly she stared back.

"Fine," he said. "One kiss and then we work."

"Just one?" Lila pouted.

His green eyes glinted at her in amusement. "It's my final offer. Take it or leave it."

"Can I take it, and then decide?"

"No."

Josh put his arms around her and kissed her gently on the lips. She kissed him back, a lot less gently. She couldn't imagine a nicer way of spending a Monday morning, kissing Josh instead of revising. Her parents would go insane, she thought happily. When they'd employed Josh, she bet they hadn't imagined him making out with their daughter.

"Lila," Josh said against her lips after several minutes. "Work."

Lila felt irritated. "You're weird, Josh. Choosing maths over kissing."

Pushing him away, she flopped down on the sofa and stared sulkily at the maths paper he'd put in front of her.

He put his hands over hers. "Look at me."

She looked up reluctantly. His lips met hers again, kissing her a lot harder than before. She gave him a swift tug, overbalancing him and pulling him down on the sofa with her, capturing his mouth firmly with hers.

This is more like it, she thought.

The more she kissed Josh, the better it seemed to get. It was quite different to the way she usually felt when she kissed a boy. Their first kiss in the roof garden had been magical, but snatching these ones right under her parents' noses were better.

"You'll be the end of me," Josh said against her lips as they kissed and kissed some more. "I'll get the sack."

"Fine by me," Lila said, tilting her head to kiss him again. "Your tutoring stinks."

The study door opened. Josh leaped up from the sofa so fast that Lila almost rolled off and hit the floor. With a thrill of terror in her belly, she saw her father standing in the doorway. He would go completely *nuts* about this.

She braced herself for the fallout before realising something odd. Her father wasn't looking furious. If anything, he looked amused.

"Mr Murray!" Josh said, looking horror-struck. He straightened his shirt collar, which had twisted round. "I'm very sorry, sir, we got a little distracted. . ."

"So I see," her dad remarked. "Glad to see everything's going so well."

And he shut the door again with a gentle click.

There was a long pause. Lila felt like the world had just tilted on its axis. Why had the bomb not fallen?

"That," Josh said, sitting down hard on the sofa beside her, "was officially the most embarrassing thing that's ever happened to me. I can't believe your father caught us kissing like that."

Strong emotions were buffeting Lila around. Her father's reaction made no sense. Why hadn't he flipped? There was only one explanation, and she found she didn't like it one bit.

"Dad likes you," she said.

Josh stopped polishing his glasses and set them on his nose again. "How do you work that one out?"

Lila stood up and paced to the far side of the study, wrapping her arms around herself. "He didn't kick you out," she said. "He didn't shout at me. He did nothing."

"That's good," Josh said with a frown. "Right?"

There was a knock. Lila's mother smiled around the study door at them.

"Sorry to interrupt. Would you both like something to drink? There's cold lemonade in the kitchen. You've been working for almost two hours now."

Her mother was looking at Josh like he was the prize turkey she'd just won in some Christmas raffle. This was getting worse. Lila could see it now. Her dad racing off to tell her mum what a lovely sensible nerdy boyfriend Lila had finally found for herself. Celebrating with cold lemonade.

"We're fine, thanks Mum," she said. "Josh is leaving in a minute."

"That would be lovely, Mrs Murray," said Josh. "Thank you very much."

Lila followed Josh out of the study towards the kitchen.

What's with the sucking up? she thought. It made her nervous.

Her dad was in the kitchen, waiting for them. There were biscuits on the table. Both her parents were smiling, she noted with disgust.

"I want to apologize again about the . . . ummm," started Josh awkwardly. "We were supposed to be studying, I know. It won't happen again."

"It was the end of the tutoring session, or almost," said Lila's dad. He poured out some lemonade and pushed it across the kitchen table towards Josh. "I know you two have been studying hard. I've seen Lila's work. You've wrought wonders already."

"You're a good influence, Josh," Lila's mother said. "If you two want to see each other, we just wanted to say that's fine by us."

Lila wanted to shrivel up like a slug in the sun. She drained her glass in one go and slammed it down on the table.

"Can we go?" she said.

Josh looked at her, his eyes questioning. She refused to return his gaze.

Her father waved them out of the kitchen. "See you in a while." He winked at Josh. "And I'll remember to knock next time."

Lila followed Josh silently back to the study. As he shut the door, the anger welled out of her like lava from a volcano.

"Did you hear yourself in there?" she hissed. "Yes Mr Murray, thank you Mrs Murray, three bags full Mr Murray. Josh, you practically kissed their *feet*."

He looked startled. "Lila, they're your parents. Of course I was polite! I—"

"I've never been more embarrassed, ever!" Lila said furiously. "That wink Dad gave you . . . urgh! It makes my skin crawl."

Josh looked wary. "I know what you're doing, Lila. Stop it."

"I want you to leave," Lila said, trembling with the violence of her emotions. "I don't want to see you any more."

"Are you serious? Because of your parents?" He tried to take her hands. "We're great together, Lila. You know we are, deep down. Don't push me away. Don't rebel for the sake of it. Is it such a bad thing that your parents approve of me?"

Lila could hardly put into words what a bad thing it was. "I . . . you . . . it's my life Josh, not theirs!" she managed, wrenching her hands away from him. "And I don't need you to tell me how to live it. This has been a massive mistake. We don't fit. I mean, look at you! And look at me! We're into different things, we have different values, *everything*. You must see that."

"You say you don't want your parents to control

your life, but you're ending this because of your parents," he said. "That's allowing them to control you just the same. Stop thinking about them for one minute and answer me this. What do *you* want?"

Lila had the sensation that she was standing close to some kind of abyss. What she said next would change everything. She shook her head, trying to dislodge the feeling that this might just be the worst decision she would ever make.

"I don't do sense, Josh," she said. "Haven't you worked that out yet? If I say I want you to leave, then *I want you to leave*."

He looked pale. "Fine. Have it your way. But know this, Lila. We are *not* a mistake."

TWENTY

"But why?" said Lila's mum, clearly bewildered by the sudden turn of events. "You were getting on so well!"

You *were getting on so well, you mean*, Lila thought. Why couldn't her parents trust her on this? They never trusted her on *anything*. She knew how she felt.

"I don't want him here," she repeated.

"What about your studies?"

"I'll do it by myself. Two hours a day for the rest of the holidays."

"Lila," said her father, "Josh is the best thing that's happened to this family in a long time. You've been settled and happy and working hard. It's taken the pressure off your mum and me. I've had a lot on at work lately, and it's made a real difference knowing Josh was taking care of you. Can't you give him another chance?"

Lila felt hot with misery and anger. "I'll do the work myself," she insisted. "I don't need tutoring any more, Dad."

Her father should have been pleased, she thought. She was saving him money, wasn't she? She felt a little twist of guilt as she remembered Josh's words on his first day of tutoring. *I need the money. I'm saving for my future.*

He shouldn't have been such a suck-up then, should he? she thought resentfully. *Then none of this would have happened.*

Her father exchanged glances with her mother. "Two hours a day for the rest of this week," he said. "You have to promise to do that, Lila. I want you back at school on Monday, fully prepared for the term's work."

Lila felt a wave of relief. She wouldn't have to face Josh again for a few days. The rest of the week would be boring, but she would get her head down and work. She wouldn't let herself think about Josh at all.

In a fit of resolve that night, she deleted Josh's number from her phone, turned it off and slid it into a drawer in her desk. At once, she felt freer. No calls, no texts. She didn't want to talk to anyone.

For the rest of the week, she poured all of her energies into her revision. She didn't even check her email. Josh may have been wrong about him and her, but he'd been right about pretty much everything else. She had to ace this term and set up some kind of future for herself if it killed her.

Her resolve weakened on Friday night. She was bored stiff, she realized, and needed a distraction.

Rhi called almost as soon as she switched on her phone. "Hey, what have you been up to, Miss Mysterious? Kissing Josh all day long?"

"We split up," Lila said shortly.

"What?" Rhi sounded genuinely shocked. "But . . . but your date went perfectly!"

Lila switched her phone to her other ear. "Rhi, I'm very grateful to you and the others for giving us such a great meal last weekend. But everything that followed was a mistake. Please trust me on that."

"I'm gutted," Rhi moaned. "The others are going to be gutted too. We really thought—"

"I wish everyone would stop thinking," Lila interrupted. "It doesn't help. I need a distraction this weekend. Do you want to meet up?"

"Ollie's organizing an all-day beach picnic tomorrow. It's on Facebook, didn't you see it?"

Lila opened Facebook and scrolled through to the details. Her spirits were lifting already. This was just what she needed: good, uncomplicated fun. She checked the invitations, just in case. Josh wasn't there.

It won't do any harm to check, she thought.

"Has anyone invited Josh, Rhi?"

"Parties aren't really Josh's style. You know that. Why," Rhi's voice changed, "do you want us to invite him?"

"No," said Lila at once. "The party plans look great. I'll be there."

"Awesome. We've missed you."

Lila felt tears pricking at the back of her throat. "I've missed you too, Rhi. See you tomorrow."

*

Saturday was clear and warm. Lila arranged all of her work folders neatly on her desk, ready for Monday morning. She allowed herself a brief moment to admire what she'd achieved.

Not so stupid after all, she told herself. She'd proved that she didn't need Josh in her life.

She pulled on her favourite denim cut-offs, a stripy long-sleeved top and her red Converse, pulled her hair loosely up on top of her head and did her make-up. It was the first time she'd bothered in almost a week, and she took extra care. Then she headed out into the sunlight to join the others at the beach.

Streams of people were moving steadily down the sand towards the path that led to their favourite cove.

"Lila!" Eve ran towards her down the path, Rhi and Polly following close behind. "Where have you *been*?"

"Off-grid," Lila said, laughing at the faces gathered around her. "You ought to try it. It totally clears your head."

She saw Ollie waving at them by the campfire. Max was there too, looking sullen. As Lila clocked

Brody Baxter sitting to one side of the flickering flames with his head bent over his guitar, she could guess why.

"Rhi told us about Josh," said Polly, hugging her tightly and dragging her towards the campfire. "You are an idiot, you know. You guys are so perfect for each other. It's written a mile high above your heads."

Lila held up her hand in warning. "Don't go there, Polly. Please. It's over and that's that. What's done is done and I'm here to have fun."

Brody strummed a chord. "What's done is done," he sang, "and I'm here to have fun. . ."

"He makes everything into a tune," said Rhi, smiling fondly at Brody.

Max looked a little sourer and moved away from the fire. He clearly hadn't forgiven Rhi and Brody yet. Lila wondered if he ever would.

The crowd suddenly parted. Lila's heart lurched to see a familiar figure sitting on the rocks, sketchbook on his knee.

Josh isn't supposed to be here, she thought anxiously.

"Who invited him?" she demanded, whirling around to face her friends.

Polly raised her hand timidly in the air. "I did. I'm sorry, but I think you should give him another chance. He really cares about you, Lila."

Lila felt furious. "Polly, this is none of your business. I told Rhi what happened. I asked *specifically* if Josh was coming and she said no. And now you say you invited him on purpose?"

"Don't be angry with her, Lila," said Eve. "She only wants what's best for you. We all do."

"Well, you have a funny way of showing it," said Lila. Her party mood was dipping faster than a roller coaster.

"Well," said Rhi diplomatically, "if you don't want to go out with him, it doesn't mean you can't be friends with him."

"I can't be friends with my exes. It's just too . . . weird."

"You managed it with Ollie," Polly said. "Please be friends, Lila. I'd hate for our group to get split up over this."

Lila glanced at Josh again. An unexpected feeling

of shame stole through her as she remembered the way she had behaved towards him. One minute they had been kissing; the next she had ordered him out of the house. She thought of his comic strip, still stuck above her bed. Maybe she didn't want to go out with him, but did she want him out of her life completely?

"Go and talk to him," Rhi coaxed.

Josh glanced up from his sketchbook. Lila realized with a stab of horror that he'd seen her.

"You can't ignore him now," said Eve.

Eve had a point. "Fine. I'm going to talk to him," said Lila. "Wish me luck."

She walked over to Josh, horribly aware of her watching friends.

"Hey," she said awkwardly.

"Hey yourself."

He was looking cute today, in rolled-up jeans and a crumpled shirt. Lila folded her arms. She felt she needed the protection. She cast around a little desperately for something to say.

"Having fun?" she said at last.

"What do you think?"

"Parties aren't usually your thing," she said, ploughing through the silence.

He was looking steadily at her, his hands resting on his sketchbook. "You don't have to talk to me. To be honest, I'd prefer it if you didn't."

Lila struggled for a reponse. "Oh," she managed.

Josh shrugged. "That's just the way I feel."

This really was an uncomfortable conversation. Lila found herself yearning for the way they had always been so easy around each other.

"I'm sorry it ended between us the way it did," she said hesitantly. "But it was for the best, Josh. We're too different, you and me. It was better to end it quickly."

"Was it?"

His eyes looked heavy, Lila realized. Like he hadn't been sleeping too well.

"Can't we go back to being friends?" she blurted.

"No," he said. "I don't think we can."

Lila was surprised by how upset she felt. Did he have to be so blunt?

"The thing is," he went on, "I really care about you.

I'm not sure I can just be friends with you any more. We nearly had something special, Lila. I hope one day you'll be able to see that."

"Right," Lila whispered. She swallowed back the tears she could feel at the back of her throat. "OK."

Not sure what else to do, she headed back to the campfire. It was a lonely walk.

"Bad, huh?" said Rhi.

Lila nodded, feeling shaky. "Pretty bad."

Eve was checking a message on her phone. "I have to go," she said, getting up.

"Everything OK?" asked Polly.

"Daddy's just asking me to go home, that's all," Eve replied. "I haven't seen him for days."

"I'll come with you," said Lila, seizing the opportunity for escape.

"But Lila, you only just got here!" Polly said.

Suddenly all Lila wanted was to get away from the beach. It was too difficult, being near Josh right now. "Sorry Polly. See you tomorrow maybe. I'll call you."

Eve was already walking quickly towards the path,

her bag swinging on her shoulder. Lila hurried to catch her up.

"Are you walking home?"

"Paulo's picking me up by the clock tower. I'm sorry, Lila, but I have to rush. Daddy's message sounded urgent." Eve hugged Lila briefly. "Talk to you tomorrow, OK?"

Lila walked home alone. She felt utterly flat, like all the energy had been sucked out of her. The awful conversation with Josh played over and over in her head. *We nearly had something special, Lila. I hope one day you'll be able to see that.* She wished her brain had a mute button.

Wearily she let herself into the house.

Her father was pacing up and down the hall with his phone pressed to his ear. "Yup," he said. "Uh-huh. Yes, has to be done. I'll meet you at the Somerstown house in ten."

Lila froze where she was. The Somerstown house?

"Hi love," said her dad, noticing her as he slid his phone into his pocket. He looked curiously grim.

"Is everything OK at Eve's place, Dad?" Lila asked, suddenly on high alert.

"Police business." He took his jacket from the hall stand and pulled it on. "I have to go out. Not sure when I'll be back. Tell your mother I'll be late, just in case."

TWENTY-ONE

Lila had a very bad feeling about this. The urgent message from Eve's dad. Now police phone calls about Eve's house. She caught her father's arm, determined not to let him leave until she understood what was happening.

"Dad, what's going on with Eve?"

He dropped a distracted kiss on her head. "I can't tell you, love. I'm sorry."

"Eve's my friend," Lila said, still holding on to her father's jacket. "You have to tell me something."

He hesitated. "All I'll say is that Eve is going to need a friend," he said. "And very soon."

With a click of the door, he was gone. Moments later, the sound of a police siren cut through the afternoon as he drove towards the town centre.

Lila sat down very suddenly on the bottom step. Fragments of the past few weeks tumbled through her head, arranging themselves into a pattern as they fell. The half-finished shopping centre they had explored not so long ago. Mr Somerstown's lapsed membership at the London club. The yachts, the cars, the staff. *I think Daddy's having money troubles.*

Lila pulled herself out of her thoughts. Eve needed her.

She ran out of the house, slamming the door behind her. At least part of the way to Eve's house was downhill. Lila concentrated, pumping her arms, swerving around corners and leaping over kerbs. Sweat pricked on her brow. Her father . . . Eve's father. . .

She put on an extra burst of speed through the Old Town, taking a sharp left up the hill by the market. The sirens were sounding louder, the closer she got to her destination. Lila had to pause, leaning against the wall of a house, fighting for breath. The road here was steep.

Eve needs you, she thought. *Keep running.*

Four police cars stood outside the Somerstown mansion, their sirens whirling silently. Blue, blue, blue.

Lila pushed through the gathering crowd: journalists, police officers, official-looking men and women in high-visibility jackets. The crackle of walkie-talkies, the flash of cameras.

A burly police officer stepped towards her. "Stay back, please, miss."

Lila tried to push past him, but it was like barging a brick wall.

"Where's Eve?" she said. "Where's my friend, Eve Somerstown?"

"There are officers with the family, miss. Please stay back."

There was a sudden burst of activity at the top of the porticoed steps that led to Eve's large front door. Lila saw her father with another officer. Mr Somerstown stood between them, his shoulders sagging. Handcuffs glinted on his wrists.

Like she was watching a film in slow motion, Lila saw them moving down the steps. Photographers were firing flashes all around her. Journalists were shouting questions.

"Mr Somerstown, do you know why you've been arrested?"

"Can you confirm that Somerstown Developments is in financial difficulties?"

"It's being alleged that you have defrauded your investors, Mr Somerstown. Would you care to comment?"

Lila hardly recognized her father, his face hard and set as he guided Mr Somerstown down the steps to the waiting police car with its silently flashing lights.

"Mind your head, sir," she heard him say as Mr Somerstown ducked into the back seat of the car.

"This is a mistake!" screeched a voice at the front door.

As one, the crowd turned and stared as Mrs Somerstown came running down the steps. Her eyes looked wild. Her hair, normally pinned to the back of her neck in a chic and expensive knot, was tumbling around her shoulders. She looked almost as young as Eve.

"Leave my husband alone!" she screeched. Photographers snapped gleeful pictures. "Take your hands off him this instant!"

"I'm sorry, Mrs Somerstown, but we have our orders," said a police officer, holding her back from her husband. "He will have access to a lawyer at the police station. Now if you don't mind, we have a job to do."

Mrs Somerstown continued to screech like a barn owl. It was painful to watch. Where was Eve? More importantly, how was she taking the arrest of her beloved father?

"Come to gloat, have you?"

Eve was advancing down the steps, her eyes fixed on Lila with loathing.

"Eve, I'm so sorry," Lila said, trying to push past the police officer again to hug her friend. "This must be awful. Is there anything I can—"

"How dare you come here?" Eve's eyes were red with weeping. "How can your father do this to us?"

Lila tried to defend herself. "I don't know what's going on, Eve. . ."

Eve's voice was rising. Lila realized she was close to breaking point. "You must really be laughing about this. Did your dad tell you to make friends with me so you could spy on us?"

"No, that's not—"

Eve gave a shriek of misery, reaching out to claw at Lila with her fingers like a cat. "I hate you," she screamed. "You've ruined my father's life. You've ruined MY life! I'll never forgive you for this, Lila. Never!"

Feeling scared now, Lila stepped back. "Of course Dad didn't tell me to be your friend. If anything, he warned me away from you," she said helplessly. "Eve, I swear I don't know anything about this!"

"Get away from me," Eve hissed.

She clenched up her hand and threw something at Lila. Lila's cheek flared with pain. She clapped her hand to her face and caught the little cat brooch with rhinestone eyes.

"I hope you choke on it," Eve snarled. "I'm going to ruin you for this, Lila Murray. *I'm going to ruin you.*"

TWENTY-TWO

Her cheek was still throbbing. Lila pressed her fingers to the cat-brooch scratch on her face. It had mostly healed, but her cheekbone felt tender to the touch. A painful reminder of the awfulness of yesterday. Her eyes felt itchy and tired. She hadn't slept well. She'd turned off her phone and put it into a drawer, trying to relish the sense of freedom just as she had done the previous week. But she felt awful. She couldn't face talking to anyone right now about what had happened. What exactly would she say?

"Sure, Dad arrested Eve's father yesterday, but it's no big deal. . ."

It was a *massive* deal. Her father's job had never affected her life like this before.

It was almost twenty-four hours since the crowd had made a sudden surge backwards to allow the police car and Mr Somerstown to exit the driveway and head towards the police station, pushing Lila back with them. She had looked back at the house just in time to see a police officer escorting Eve, Chloe and their hysterical mother back inside the house and closing the door. Two guards had taken up position by the pillars, guarding the inhabitants, walkie-talkies prominently on display. There had been nothing for it but to walk back home.

Lila cast her mind back, thinking hard about the clues she had been too blind to see. Ryan had mentioned rumours of fraud at Eve's party, the day he had died. *You're as big a fraud as your father, Eve Somerstown.* Eve had silenced him with an invitation to stay at the party, which he had gatecrashed. Why hadn't she paid more attention at the time? Then there was her father's strange overreaction to her wanting to spend a day with Eve in London. And now all the hideousness of that very public arrest. Her father had put her in an impossible situation and she hated him for it. She didn't want to know what her friends were thinking right now. Then she remembered Josh and how she'd blown everything with him. She was filled with regret.

Lila's heart twisted with misery for Eve. Her friend's life was being destroyed, and there was nothing she could do about it. Except Eve wasn't her friend any more. She was her mortal enemy. Again.

Her dad hadn't been back to the house yet. Lila was glad. She was so angry, she had no idea what she would say when she next saw him.

After a fitful night, she had spent most of Sunday pacing her room, reading news updates as they flashed up on her laptop. SOMERSTOWN ARREST: LATEST DEVELOPMENTS scrolled endlessly across her screen. MAYOR OF HEARTSIDE BAY ACCUSED OF EMBEZZLING INVESTMENT FUNDS. It was impossible to stop watching.

The sky outside her window had darkened almost without her noticing. She looked dully at the clock on her bedside table. Almost ten o'clock.

School tomorrow, she thought.

She groaned and flopped back on the bed, covering her eyes with the heels of her hands. She slept.

Someone was knocking, somewhere. Lila peeled open her eyes groggily and sat up. She was still dressed, she realized. What was the time? More importantly, who was knocking?

Yawning, she opened her bedroom door. No one was there. In slight disbelief, she headed for the window and peered out.

Josh was standing on her garage roof.

"Josh?" she said, looking down at him in stupefaction.

"I want you to come with me," he said.

Lila was suddenly wide awake. "It must be nearly midnight. What are you doing on my garage roof?"

He was reaching both his hands towards her. "Take my hand and come out here. It's perfectly safe."

"I know it's safe," she said, looking out at the moonlit road beyond the small front garden. "I've used it myself a few times. But that doesn't explain what you're doing here."

"You weren't answering your phone," said Josh. "I had no choice. I had to see you."

Lila rubbed her eyes. "Go home, Josh," she said.

"I'm poison. I seem to hurt everyone I get close to. Don't let me hurt you any more than I already have."

"I'm willing to take that risk." His eyes gleamed in the moonlight. "Now are you going to start climbing, or am I going to have to come up there and get you?"

"Why are you doing this?" she said helplessly. "Can't it wait?"

He seemed to find this funny. "Definitely not. Are you coming?"

Lila grabbed a fleece and pulled it around her shoulders, took Josh's outstretched hand and wriggled out to join him on the roof. They jumped down to the grass below, which was soft and spongy and cushioned their fall.

"What's going on, Josh?" Lila begged as he pulled her out into the street. "I don't understand any of this. I thought you didn't want to be friends."

"I don't," he said.

He said nothing else for a while. Lila was too confused and tired to talk. She let him pull her onwards, down towards the town, past the station, right down to the beach itself.

"OK," she said slowly, looking around the silent sands. "We're here because. . .?"

He put his arm around her shoulders and pointed with his free hand. "Look," he said.

Lila followed his pointing finger towards Kissing Island. The causeway was uncovered, the sand gleaming pale in the moonlight.

"I've never seen that before," she said in wonder.

He took her hand again. "Walk with me?"

Lila did as she was told. The sandy pathway beckoned them, shining like silver. It was a full moon, she realized.

"What's the time?" she asked. Her voice felt shaky.

Josh squeezed her hand more tightly. "If you need to ask, you haven't been living in Heartside Bay for long enough."

Feeling as if she was in a dream, Lila glanced back at the clock tower's illuminated face, just visible from the pathway they were on. Two minutes until midnight.

You can only walk to it when the tides are just right. . . If you kiss your true love on Kissing Island at midnight of a full moon, you will be together for ever. . .

Suddenly something inside her stilled to nothing. She was meant to be here. She knew it as surely as she knew the feeling of Josh's hand in hers. She didn't know why she'd ever doubted her feelings for him, why she'd pushed him away.

They walked hand in hand along the silver pathway until they reached the tiny beach of Kissing Island. The moon watched with its great white eye as Josh stopped at the water's edge. He pushed his hands through Lila's hair and cupped her face, tilting it towards him.

"Sometimes, you need to be in the moment," he said. "Right?"

Lila nodded wordlessly.

"This is the moment."

The clock tower chimed midnight as he touched her lips with his, bringing his arms around her and pulling her close. Lila melted against him, kissing him back with everything she had. All the kisses she had ever experienced were nothing to this one. Nothing at all. For ever suddenly seemed like a possibility.

"You know," she said, pulling back to catch her breath, "love isn't so bad when it's right."

"You talk too much," said Josh. "Kiss me again."

She did.